THE COMPANY OF GHOSTS

Berlie Doherty

WINNER OF THE CARNEGIE MEDAL

ANDERSEN PRESS

First published in 2013 by
Andersen Press Limited
20 Vauxhall Bridge Road
London SW1V 2SA
www.andersenpress.co.uk

British Library Cataloguing in Publication Data available.

ISBN 978 1 84939 729 2

Printed and bound by CPI Group (UK) Ltd, Croydon, CR0 4YY

THE COMPANY OF GHOSTS

Are you trying to be brave or crying to be saved?

Niklas Schütte

For my good friend Dolores, who probably
doesn't believe in ghosts.

And with thanks to David and Jane Brown,
who shared their love of an island with me;
to Lisa Daniels, who shared her love of lighthouses;
and to Ruth Knowles, Charlie Sheppard and
Eloise Wilson, who devoted such editorial
care to my manuscript.

CHAPTER ONE

The island is shrouded in mist. A girl stands so close to the water that spray showers over her like beads of pearl. Yet she feels nothing.

She is watching a fisherman drawing into land. He beaches his boat and hauls a basket out onto a shore that is purple with the shells of mussels. He crouches down, scooping handfuls into his basket. He whistles tunefully as he works, intent on his task. He doesn't hear any sound as the girl steps over the shell beach towards him, nor does he see a shadow as she stands between him and the low sunlight. He doesn't hear her voice. He hears only the clattering of the shells, the scraping of waves on the shingle, the sobbing cry of gulls.

'Guthrie,' the girl says to him, as she says every time he comes to the island. 'Please help me. Will you never help me?'

He pauses for a moment, glances up as if something caught his senses, and then frowns. He finishes his task quickly, heaves his basket into his boat *Miss Tweedie*, and heads for home with the tide.

CHAPTER TWO

Ellie waited until she heard her mother and Angus head up to their room. Time to go. Quickly she fished out her father's rucksack from under the bed and stuffed a few items of clothing inside it, then looked round the room, dithering. On top of her desk were her sketchbook and art materials, all unused. They had been a last gift from her father. Hastily she gathered them up and slid them behind the little bundle of clothes in the rucksack. Her mother's voice, movement in the other room, a quick laugh. *Now*, Ellie told herself. *Go. Go.* She had already written a note and placed it on her pillow. *I can't come with you. Enjoy yourselves.*

She crept down the stairs and out into the front garden. She felt dizzy, as if she hadn't breathed properly all day. But she daren't stop now. She ran along the street and didn't pause until she had reached a bus stop on the corner, where she wouldn't be seen from the house, then took out her phone and rang her friend, Hannah. There was no reply. She walked on to the next bus stop, dialling one of her other friends on the way. Again, only voicemail. There was no point in leaving a message. After all, what could she say to them, but 'Help me'?

Ellie wriggled her father's rucksack from her shoulders and let it slouch down to the ground as she felt in her pockets; a half-eaten bar of chocolate in one, her purse in the other. She tipped out a handful of loose change into her palm and counted the coins. Hardly anything there. Her bank card was no use as her account was empty. She stared ahead blankly as the traffic rumbled past, calculating how long her money would last, and was startled out of her reverie by a voice behind her.

'Where's your violin? Not coming to orchestra today?'

A tall, smiling girl with a cello strapped to her back had joined her at the bus stop. For a moment Ellie couldn't remember her name. She hardly knew her, except that they both played in the strings section of the city youth orchestra. The other girl was the lead cellist, a much better player than Ellie would ever be, and even took solo parts sometimes. Ellie always sat in the second section of the violins, feverishly sight-reading because she never practised the music despite her mother's threats and her father's bribes. Yet she loved orchestra, loved the kind of music they played, and wouldn't normally miss the practice for anything. But that night she'd forgotten all about it, forgotten everything except her own anger and unhappiness. It would have been somewhere to go, wouldn't it? Something to do to get her out of the house. But then what?

'Going away?' the tall girl asked. Morag, that was it. Morag Donaldson. When she played her cello her whole body swayed, and her hair swung with her like a shining black veil. She would have her head high and her eyes closed, as if she were playing in her dreams. She hardly ever needed to look at the music.

Ellie nodded and glanced up the road again, as if she were anxiously waiting for the bus to come. *Go away*, she thought. *Just leave me alone.*

'Somewhere nice?'

Ellie started crying, tears just rolling down her cheeks as she stood, silent and helpless, doing nothing to try to stop them.

'I'm sorry.' Morag nervously shifted her weight from one leg to another. Then, 'Please don't, Ellie.' And then, rummaging in her pocket, 'Here, have some tissues.' And last of all, 'What's the matter?'

The bus arrived. The doors opened and it stood, shivering, until it was clear that the girls weren't getting on, then the doors closed again and it pulled away.

'You've missed your bus,' sniffed Ellie.

'So've you.'

'It doesn't matter.' Ellie screwed up the tissue into a ball of pulp in her fist and shoved it into her pocket. 'I don't think I wanted that one.'

'It's the only one that goes from here,' Morag reminded her gently. 'Where do you want to get to?'

Ellie looked away and stared at the leaning post of the bus stop as if it was the only thing she wanted to talk to. 'I've no idea. Anywhere.'

There was a long silence. Morag watched helplessly as Ellie struggled against her tears. She was such a waif of a girl, such a tiny, white-faced picture of unhappiness. 'I know it's none of my business, but are you running away from home or something?'

'Not running away,' Ellie muttered. 'I just walked out, that's all.'

'And you've really no idea where you're going? I mean, where will you stop tonight?'

A boy on a rattling bike swerved onto the pavement in front of them, wove between Ellie's rucksack and the bus stop, grinning at each of the girls in turn, then bounced off the pavement again and sped away.

'I'll be okay. I'll be fine.'

Morag shook her head. 'You aren't okay. You're upset. You can't just go off on your own like this. Terrible things happen to girls of our age when they run away from home. Rape, murder, drugs, prostitution . . .' She spread out her hands. 'Sorry, I'm sounding like my mum. But – Ellie. You mustn't.'

Her earnestness gave Ellie a weak smile. 'I won't let anything happen. I'm not stupid.'

'Please go back home, just for tonight. Why won't you?'

Ellie hesitated. She didn't want to tell any of her story. She couldn't bear to tell anyone. Not yet. But Morag's concern was like a warm red scarf on a chilly night. 'My dad's not there any more,' she said simply. That would do. That was bad enough. And, anyway, it was the worst thing.

'Tell you what. If you like, you could come back to my house for a bit. Have you had anything to eat tonight?'

Ellie shrugged, overwhelmed again. She couldn't remember when she'd last eaten. There had been food after the awful ceremony that morning, she remembered, but she hadn't touched any of it. She'd spent the rest of the day dry-eyed in her room, staring into space, and had finally hunted out her father's rucksack and bunched those few things into it. And then, she had simply walked out of the house.

She was dimly aware that Morag had turned away from her and was rapidly texting. Ellie bent down to pick up her rucksack again, thinking that maybe she should walk to the railway station. At least she would be out of the wind there.

Morag pushed the mobile into her pocket and swung round to her. 'Mum's fixing you something to eat. And me. I'm starving,' she laughed. 'Just come round and eat something. It'll help you think.'

'I can't.' Ellie stared helplessly at Morag. Really, at that moment, no-one could offer her anything more comforting. And yet they hardly knew each other.

'Why not?'

'What about orchestra?'

'What about it? It's Strauss this month anyway. I can't stand those Viennese waltzes. Too cheerful for me!' Morag helped Ellie to ease her rucksack onto her shoulders. 'My mum's brilliant, by the way. She won't ask you any questions. She might offer you a bed for the night, though. Think about it.' She didn't add that her mother was a social worker, and well used to dealing with distressed teenagers. She stood back and smiled at Ellie. 'Oh, and my dad's just a big clumsy bear who only thinks about poetry. He might not even notice you!'

Ellie realised three things. She was very hungry. She didn't even have enough loose change for a bag of chips. And she was suddenly bone tired.

Ellie had never seen a house in such a state of gentle chaos before. Her own house was stylish, calm, cream and immaculately ordered. The only splashes of colour came from her father's paintings, and they had been removed recently and replaced with mirrors artfully positioned to reflect light from the windows and the different greens from the garden. In Morag's house the sagging armchairs were covered with cheerful Indian throws and cushions. Where they had slipped out of place to reveal the fabric underneath you could see the draggled threads where generations of cats had clawed and snagged the material. Books jostled for shelf space with photographs, CDs, a hairbrush wispy with grey hair, a ball of yellow knitting wool with needles sticking out like a snail's horns, biros, bunches of keys and sea shells. An amber cat stretched out, full-length, on the windowsill, trapping to itself the only smear of sunshine that was left of the day.

Morag led Ellie through to the kitchen, where her mother was easing slices of pie onto a couple of non-matching plates. She glanced up at Ellie and smiled.

'Hi, Ellie. I'm Sheila. Just drop your bag on the floor. Gosh, you're like your mum.'

Ellie was dismayed. 'Oh. You know her.'

'A bit. Angela Brockhole. Very elegant. I've seen her at your concerts a few times, and we went to the same yoga class for a bit. We used to go for coffee afterwards, with a few others from the class, but I never get a chance to go these days. The number of classes I join and never finish! You don't forget a name like yours though. Badger sett it means, but of course you'd know that. Now – eat!'

She pointed to a chair. Ellie slid down into it and let her rucksack thud softly to the floor. She was too tired to say thank you. She gazed round the kitchen while Sheila rummaged in a drawer for cutlery. There was a slate board hanging on the wall next to the table, with the words *When all the world was young, lad, and all the trees were green. Kingsley* chalked on it. It was hanging slightly askew, and she resisted the temptation to reach out and straighten it.

'Aren't you eating yours, Morag? You didn't eat much tea.'

Morag shook her head. 'I've got a bit of a headache now.'

'All the more for Ellie then. Hope you're not veggie. We used to be, but we've all slipped over to the dark side. Only eat organic meat though. *Guten appetit*, Ellie.' She gestured to Morag to follow her out of the kitchen. Ellie could hear the murmur of their voices, but couldn't tune in to any of the words. She helped herself to some water, dislodging a glass from a pile of dishes soaking in a bowl of suds, and ate. She only looked up from her plate when Sheila Donaldson came back alone into the kitchen and sat at the table, phone in hand.

Isn't that typical of adults? thought Ellie. *I know exactly what's coming. She's going to phone Mum and get her to take me home.* She pushed her plate away.

'Morag's making up a bed for you in her room. It's only an airbed, but it'll be fine. And you can flop into it any time you like. You look as if that's the only thing you want to do, even though it's only just gone eight.'

Ellie felt her tears welling up, and Sheila just squeezed her hand and waited a minute before she spoke again.

'I'm going to phone your mother now. I just want her to know you're safe. I don't want to know anything about what's happened between you. It's none of my business. But if my beautiful sixteen-year-old daughter had just walked out of the house, I'd want to know where she was. Okay?'

Sheila slid a pad and pen towards her. Ellie nodded and sighed. 'I'm going to tell her you're asleep,' she said, when Ellie had finished. 'Which you probably will be by the time I've finished deciphering this. Off you go. The bathroom's at the top of the stairs. Sleep well, my love.'

Ellie used the bathroom and stood, uncertain, on the landing; not sure which room she should be using. She pushed open a bedroom door tentatively and backed out again in dismay when she saw the long figure of a boy stretched out on the bed, reading. He grunted without looking up.

'That's George's room,' Morag called from across the landing. 'I'm in here, Ellie.'

Ellie closed the door quietly and went into the opposite bedroom, where Morag was unrolling a sleeping bag onto an airbed.

'Thanks for doing this,' Ellie said. 'You've been really kind. You and your mum.'

'You're welcome. I've got a bit of packing to do now. I'll try not to disturb you though. I can do some of it in my brother's room.'

'Are you going away?'

'Tomorrow, yes. We always go away as soon as the school holidays start.'

Ellie looked away, dismayed again. She clutched the strap of her rucksack. It was suddenly a bulky thing, impossible to hide, assuming unlimited hospitality. *One night*, she thought wildly. *And then what? Where do I go next?*

She noticed a large black and white photograph hanging near Morag's bed. Pretending to be casual and at ease, she went over to look more closely. It was a seascape, moody with rocks and cliffs and wild showers of spray. Her own reflection was drawn into it, like a ghost image among the lights and shadows.

'That's our island,' Morag said.

'It looks mysterious.'

'It is. That's where we're going tomorrow.'

'Is it really yours? You really own an island?'

'Well, no, we don't really. It feels like ours because no-one else ever uses it. It belongs to some distant cousin of Dad's. Guthrie. But he lives on the mainland now. He used to be the lighthouse keeper.'

'So no-one lives there any more?'

'No-one.'

Ellie leaned forward and touched the photograph

lightly. Her breath misted the glass so her reflection grew hazy and then vanished as if into cloud. Immediately she pulled herself away. She squatted on her airbed, watching Morag collecting her things together, remembering it was only a few hours since she had done just that, since she had stuffed random bits and pieces of her life into her rucksack, desperate to get away from her house.

'We've been going there as long as I can remember,' Morag continued. 'Mum keeps dropping hints about going to the Bahamas or Cornwall or even Skye for a change, but somehow we always get drawn back to the island.'

'Family holidays,' Ellie said. 'I used to enjoy those.'

'This might be our last family holiday, Mum thinks. She's been saying that since George was sixteen. She reckons we'll just be wanting to go off with our friends next year. He will, at the end of the month, but the island has to come first!' She glided round the room, chatting lightly, and Ellie let her talk wash over her, relaxing and soothing. She felt easy now in Morag's company. She slid down into her sleeping bag and lay with her head on one side so she could see the photograph of the island.

'You're so lucky,' she said. 'Having an island to go to.'

'I know. It's brilliant.'

'When Dad was here we used to go to England. Near Newcastle. All his family lived there. But they're all dead now.' Her voice trembled slightly.

'Oh God, that's awful for you. I'm so sorry.' Morag looked at her, anxious in case Ellie was going to cry again, then tried to brighten her tone. 'Newcastle. That's where George is going next year. Newcastle Uni. Mum's furious with him for not choosing Aberdeen. That's where *she* comes from.' She paused with her hand on the doorjamb, ready to go downstairs. 'Ellie. What will you do tomorrow?'

Ellie shrugged. 'I'm not sure.' *I could go back home*, she thought. *Mum will have gone by then. But I'd be alone in the house for two weeks.* She bit her lip and curled herself up inside the sleeping bag, letting the day's unhappiness wash over her. 'I'll be fine.'

CHAPTER THREE

Ellie woke up the next morning to the sound of a cello being played. She lay listening to the measured, rich voice of the instrument echoing round the house. *It must be Morag, practising*, she thought. *No wonder she's so good. It would never enter my head to practise my violin at a time like this. When I go home, I'll practise every day.* And then she remembered that home was different now. Home would never be the same again.

She got up quickly, washed and dressed herself, and stood at the top of the stairs, hesitant to go down to a strange kitchen without being invited. She heard someone moving in one of the other bedrooms, a radio being turned on, a man clearing his throat in the bathroom. She tiptoed down the stairs, not sure now which room was the kitchen anyway. She heard someone clattering dishes and pushed open the door. Sheila Donaldson was in there, bright as sunshine.

'Ellie! Good morning! Sleep well? Come on in, sit down, help yourself to anything you want,' she said. 'I'm rushing about as usual, but everyone else takes their time. You get started and I'll go and drag Morag away from her cello. Oh, by the way, your mother came round last night, when you were asleep. It was nice to see her again, actually.'

Ellie nodded. She tried to keep her voice level. 'What did she say?'

'Well, she was very concerned about you, naturally. She told me what's happened, and of course she knows why you're so upset. I haven't told Morag any of this, by the way; she was up in George's room when your mother was here. But she does know that your mother is going away for two weeks, and so she's come up with an idea. I phoned your mum back about it early this morning and she's very happy if you are. But she wants to speak to you about it.'

'About what?'

'Going away. So here . . .' She held out the phone. 'Phone her, Ellie.'

Ellie shook her head, confused. Did they want her to go away with her mother after all? 'I can't. Not yet.'

'Ellie. She's your mother. She's worried about you.'

'I'll text her.'

'Talk to her.'

Reluctantly Ellie keyed the number. Her mother's voice was anxious and strained. 'Ellie. Thank goodness you rang. We're supposed to have set off already, but I wouldn't leave the house until I'd spoken to you. I'll come over for you now, if you want.'

Ellie shook her head. She gripped the receiver tightly. 'No, Mum.'

'So you're happy with Sheila's plan?'

Ellie looked at Sheila. 'I don't know what the plan is.'

Sheila Donaldson swung round from the counter, her hand to her mouth. 'Oh my goodness! Hasn't Morag asked you yet?'

Ellie shook her head. 'I haven't seen Morag this morning—'

'Going to their island with them,' her mother interrupted, at the end of the phone line. 'Are you happy with that?'

'To the island?' Ellie looked at Sheila again. She could hardly believe what her mother was saying. 'Really?'

'Would you like to come?' Sheila asked, smiling. 'You'd be very welcome.' She put her hands together as if she were clasping them in prayer, then went out of the kitchen to leave Ellie to talk in private to her mother.

'Ellie?' Her mother again, a far-away voice, a dream

voice slipping into the distortion of a bad connection. 'Will you be all right?'

'Oh yes!' said Ellie. 'Oh yes, please.'

'Have you got enough things? You're sure you're happy about it?'

'Of course I am!'

'Then I'm happy too. Sheila's a really nice person. So kind. I know she'll look after you, if you're sure you want to do it, Ellie. Have a lovely time.' And the connection finally broke up, and her mother's voice had gone.

Ellie put the receiver down and crossed her arms tightly, hugging herself with relief and utter pleasure. She didn't have to face her mother yet; she didn't have to live in the house on her own. She was going to stay on Morag's beautiful, mysterious island.

The endless circle of music stopped, and Morag followed her mother back into the kitchen, flexing her fingers to loosen them up after playing.

'Hi, Ellie. Okay? I'm sorry I didn't get a chance to ask you about the island. You were fast asleep when I got up this morning. Is it all right?'

'I can't believe it,' Ellie said. 'You're so kind. I'd love to come, if you're sure.'

'It'll be nice for Morag to have someone else there,' Sheila said. 'Unfortunately I can't come till the weekend, because of work. George isn't much company, he'll be bird-watching all the time, won't he, Mo?'

'Dad will be writing poetry,' Morag said. 'They're not really aware of my existence, either of them. Mum, it sounds as if George is up already.'

'Miracle.' Sheila said. 'It's because of the island.'

At that moment, Morag's brother loped into the kitchen behind his father, as tall and big-boned as he was, as darkly floppy-haired and wide-eyed. He lifted his hands in a vague greeting as he passed Ellie, as if there was always a stranger sitting at the kitchen table at that time in the morning, and maybe, Ellie thought, maybe there always was in that shambling, casual household. He hauled himself onto the counter like a languid spider, draping his legs over the kitchen bin. His mother plucked out one of his earphones.

'Meet Ellie.'

'Hi, Ellie.' George plugged himself back in. 'I think we met last night.'

His father swung round from the toaster, just realising that Ellie was there. He lunged across to her and stood smiling down, arms akimbo, not sure whether to shake her hand or ruffle her hair.

'This is Bill,' Sheila said. 'Actually, his name's Stuart, but he doesn't answer to it.'

'Stuart was my uncle's name, and as I never liked the man I think of it as his alone,' Mr Donaldson explained. 'So Bill fits the bill!' He chuckled as if he'd just thought of it, but Sheila rolled her eyes resignedly.

'I believe you're coming to the island with us,' Bill said. 'Splendid.'

'Guthrie won't like it,' George muttered.

'Guthrie has his idiosyncrasies,' Sheila said. 'Just as the island does. You'll have to be prepared for that, Ellie.'

'Ellie, let me tell you, it's the most beautiful place on God's earth.' Bill beamed down at her as if he was giving her a present.

'There's no running water, no electricity, be warned! – and it's really small. Toast,' Sheila reminded her husband. 'It can feel very strange at times. Not spooky exactly,' she added, 'just – atmospheric.'

'I think it is quite spooky. But it's really beautiful,' Morag said. 'I don't want any toast, Dad.'

Bill ambled over to the slate board and rubbed out the

Charles Kingsley quote, replacing it with *My heart faints in me for the distant sea. W. de la Mare.*

'Guthrie doesn't like strangers going to the island. He's told us that,' George muttered again. He sat with his arms folded and his eyes closed, lost in the music that no-one else could hear.

'I'll sort Guthrie.' Bill caught two slices of toast and huffed across the kitchen with them as if they were setting his fingers on fire. 'Don't take any notice of George. Are you happy to risk it?'

'So it's very basic, a bit spooky, tiny, beautiful,' Ellie said. 'I can't wait to be there!'

Later, she sat in the garden watching the cats while the car was being packed. It was a wild garden, frothing with pink and white and red campion and grandmother's cap, yellow poppies like her grandfather's cottage garden in England. She imagined sitting with her father, trying to paint it, talking together about what they were seeing. Her father would probably have asked her to draw one of the cats.

'The one like marmalade. See? Same colour as the orange wing tips of the butterflies. Ginger, honey-gold, lion-coloured. Sun on his flanks – more golden there. White chin, like dandelion fluff. Full stretch, bum up. Watch its movement, flow, *catness*. Bristling whiskers. Claws stretched. Tail twitching.'

'Dad, I can't draw that. Not twitch.'

'Try, sweetheart,' her father would have said. 'You don't know till you try.'

She could hear Sheila jovially giving instructions, advice, warnings, while Bill whistled to himself and generally seemed to ignore her. Now that she was alone again, listening to the bustle and laughter of the family preparing for the holiday, Ellie felt her own excitement draining away. She didn't belong here, she didn't even know this family. She would be an intruder in their special place, a spare part, a bulky rucksack. She would never fit in with them. *How could I have been so stupid?* she thought. *They won't really want me there with them. It will be so embarrassing.* But there was no way she could get out of it now, not without offending them. Sheila would insist, Morag would be disappointed. It would seem like bad manners. Maybe it was easier to go with them than to stay behind. If she told them she didn't want to go after all, Sheila Donaldson would phone her mother, and Ellie would be back where she started yesterday. She had to go; she couldn't face the consequences of pulling out. And, deep inside those tangled thoughts, she knew that she did want to go to the island.

Maybe they were expecting her to offer to help, at least. She stood up, wiping her hands on her jeans, suddenly hot and sticky with nerves. She was just about to go back into the house when she heard George say, 'Does she really have to come with us? This might be our last holiday together. She'll be a drag.'

She froze into stillness.

'She's had a bad time. And she needs a break from her mother,' she heard Sheila reply.

'Don't we all.'

And laughter.

Ellie pressed herself against the wall, too embarrassed to move, and to her alarm Morag came out through the garage door and joined her.

'I'm a bit head-achy today,' Morag said. 'I thought I'd leave the packing to them and hide out here with you.'

'Would you rather we didn't go?' Ellie said awkwardly. 'I don't mind, honestly. In fact, I think I'd prefer to stay here . . . till your mother goes, you know.'

'I'll be fine. I'd prefer to leave it a day or two but George just won't wait. He's always like this.'

'But we don't all have to go yet, do we?' Ellie felt desperate.

'Oh, we do,' Morag laughed. 'It's the family ritual. We always go before Mum. Set it up, make it nice for her. Then she sails across like Cleopatra in her barge, as Dad always says, loaded with cakes. No, seriously, I'll be fine. We'll go today. George is really keyed up for it.'

'Yeah, I noticed.'

'I'm so glad you want to come.' Morag smiled at her. 'I'm really looking forward to it.'

'So am I,' said Ellie. *But I'm not*, she thought. *I can't imagine anything worse now. Not if George is going to be there.*

Eventually Sheila came out to the garden and hustled them to the car, pushing thermos flasks and plastic boxes of cakes and biscuits into their hands, nestling the girls in with piles of pillows and other bedding until there was hardly room for them to move. When Ellie was squeezed into her seatbelt, Sheila leaned in and handed her an old fleece and some socks and waterproofs. 'It might be an island of dreams, but the weather can be atrocious! You'll need these. We've squashed your airbed and a sleeping bag for you in the boot.'

'Thank you ever so much.' Ellie stuffed the warm clothes on top of her rucksack. *There's no getting out of it now*, she thought. 'I'm really looking forward to it.' She stared fixedly at the back of George's head.

'I'll give your mother a ring now, tell her we've packed you in. You all right, Mo? You're looking a bit pale.'

'It's just this headache, Mum. It'll clear up.'

'Time and tide will wait for no man!' Bill came out of the house, rubbing his hands together. 'And neither will cousin Guthrie.' He flung his arms round his wife. 'Parting is such sweet sorrow.'

'Oh, go on, get off with you!' Sheila mounted her bike and set off to work with a cheerful wave. 'Ellie – I need your mum's mobile number. Text it to me, will you? I'll see you at the weekend,' she shouted. 'Have fun!' She wobbled perilously onto the road.

From that moment, it seemed, things began to go badly awry. Morag sat, tense and upright, breathing deeply, eyes tight shut, saying nothing.

'You okay?' Ellie whispered. 'You've gone really pale.'

Morag didn't reply. George had his earphones in and Bill sang to himself as he drove. Ellie sat in silence, desperately shy and awkward. *What am I doing?* she asked herself. *I don't even know these people. They've all been so kind to me. Except for George. But maybe if he's permanently plugged into his iPod I'll be able to just ignore him.* She felt her mobile vibrate in her pocket and fished it out. It was a message from her mother. *No,* she decided. *I won't read it. Not yet.* She stared out of the window, watching the streets slip by. They were heading for the mountains, and beyond them, the sea. There would be nothing to cling onto, nothing familiar, nothing safe. But she would have escaped the wretchedness of being at home.

They were nearly two hours into the journey when Morag touched Ellie's arm and gestured to her that she was going to be sick. Ellie leaned forward and tapped Bill on the shoulder, and he swung into a lay-by. Morag stumbled over the rucksacks and sleeping bags that were piled round her and half-fell out of the car. She vomited immediately into the long grass.

'Are you all right?' Ellie asked. Tentatively, she put an arm round Morag's shoulders while Bill flapped about in the boot of the car trying to find tissues under the piles of packing.

George watched gloomily. 'She's always car sick.'

'It's worse than that,' his sister moaned.

'Period pains?' Ellie whispered.

'Worse.'

'She gets it bad. Dysmenorrhoea,' George said.

'Try to spell it!' Bill laughed, trying to lighten the moment. 'Diarrhoea. That's another one I can't do.'

'She hasn't got that,' George pointed out. He climbed back into the car, pretending disgust, but watched his sister anxiously all the same.

Morag was bent double now, clutching her stomach. 'Worse than anything.'

They watched her as she vomited again. Passing cars slowed down, their occupants peering out of the windows to see what was happening; white, eager faces, mouths open, eyes screwed up to miss nothing. Eventually Morag climbed back into the car and sank back into her seat. George gave her a bottle of water; Ellie found a rug in the boot and tucked it round her. Morag smiled at her feebly. Bill stooped his long body through the door, felt her forehead, and stooped out again. He stood scratching his chin thoughtfully.

'I think it could be a migraine,' he said at last. 'Sheila used to get them a lot when I first met her, but I've never known Morag to have one. The only thing for it is to go to bed in a darkened room for a few hours; sleep it off.' He bent down again. 'Would you like to do that, Mo? To sleep, perchance to dream?'

Morag nodded, closing her eyes against the daylight.

'I think she should lie down on the back seat,' Bill said. 'Would you be able to manage, Ellie, if she has her legs over your knees?'

'Of course.' Ellie scrambled back into the car and somehow managed to squeeze herself in. Morag moaned softly as Ellie tried to lift her into place.

'I hurt all over,' she mumbled.

Ellie tried to perch herself right on the edge of the seat. Now she couldn't fasten the seatbelt.

'That won't do,' Bill said. 'Out you get, Ellie. Let's try something else. And there's no room for George now, with all that extra baggage from the back piled on his seat. Why does Sheila always make us bring so much *stuff*?'

George tried to clamber in, and failed. 'I think we passed a train station not long ago,' he said. 'I could wander back there and see if it's the line that goes to Kyle.'

'It is,' Bill said. 'That's the line Mum goes on. Oh yes, I can see the station sign. Just down the road, that's lucky. Well, you could do that. The train Mum usually gets probably passes through here at about this time. Check the times on that phone of yours, George. You could go to Kyle and stop the night at Izzie's. I'll take Morag home. I think I might want the doctor to have a look at her. She might need some antihistamines or antibiotics or something. Here,' he fumbled in his wallet and handed George some notes. 'More than enough for tickets and a bit of food. We'll drive to Kyle when Morag perks up, collect the fresh supplies we need for the island, and then we'll ask Guthrie to take us all over to the island on the next tide. Sorted.'

George looked up from his smartphone. 'There's a train in twenty minutes.'

There was an uncomfortable silence. Ellie realised that Bill and George were both looking at her. 'I'll try to climb in the front,' she said, suddenly aware of the awful alternative. It was unthinkable. She hoicked everything out of the front seat and climbed in, making herself as small as possible as Bill attempted to load the bags and boxes round her. It couldn't be done. The shapes were too awkward, nothing fitted. They would never manage a two hour journey back home like that.

'I'm sorry, Ellie,' Bill said. 'It looks as if you'll have to go on the train with George. Do you mind?'

'I'll manage like this. I could look after Morag.'

'I can't drive the car with all that stuff there. There's no alternative. You can see that.'

She heard the testiness in his voice, and climbed out of the seat, spilling the contents, shoving them back in. *I'm in the way*, she thought. *This is awful. Awful.* 'Perhaps I could get the train home.'

'There isn't one,' George told her. 'Not till tonight. Mum uses this line all the time.'

'You'll be fine,' Bill assured her, relieved now, and anxious to get away. 'Kyle's a bonny wee toon, as they say over there. My sister Izzie will enjoy showing you round. And anyway, George will look after you.'

Ellie spent the train journey gazing out of the window, watching the flick of rivers and houses, gardens, fields, the rapid ticking past of other people's lives. Then the track delved into the mountains. She recited the colours to herself if she were trying to paint them. *Dun. Lavender. Green. Cobalt. Heather. What colours for heather? Dad. Dad. Help me.* George sat slouched in the seat opposite, earphones in place, eyes closed, drumming his fingertips on the table in time to the music. Eventually she was aware that he had opened his eyes and was watching her. She ran nervous fingers through her hair and bent her head. *I wish I wasn't here. Anywhere but here. Why did I do this crazy thing? I should have gone home.*

Home. But Dad's not there any more. She brushed her eyes with the back of her hand. *Dad.*

As if he had been reading her thoughts, George pulled out his earphones and left them dangling round his neck, then muttered clumsily, 'I'm sorry about your father.'

'Oh. Thanks.'

'When did he die?'

Ellie was startled. 'Die? He's not dead.'

It was an awful moment, simmering with embarrassment and pain. George flushed, groaned, put his hands over his face and muttered into the cave he'd made with his fingers. 'Oh God. What an idiot. Morag told me last night that you were upset because you had lost your dad, and I thought she meant he'd died. Oh God, I'm sorry. What an awful thing to say. I'm really sorry!'

The train was pulling into a station. People were standing up, lifting luggage down from racks, moving down the aisle.

'He's gone to England. Cornwall.'

George huffed, relieved. 'Right. Not so bad, then.'

Isn't it? Ellie thought. *Isn't it really?* She let out her breath slowly. She had never talked about the pain of his leaving to anyone. 'He – well, he left us. I didn't want him to go.'

'It's rotten for you. But – well, things will get better.

In time.' He smiled at her shyly, then stood up. 'Actually, we're here, you know.' He stretched up to get both of their rucksacks, stooped to peer out of the windows again. 'Tide's in! Can you see? I bet Guthrie's there now. We can go today. Straight to the island!'

CHAPTER FOUR

'Wild Island. It's out there, somewhere,' George said.

'Is it really called that?'

'It really is. Great name, isn't it?'

Ellie stood a few paces behind him. Beneath her feet the sea splashed against the wooden stanchions of the jetty, heaving darkly between the planks. She could hear the crinkle of waves across the white shell-sand, the slow shift as they crawled ceaselessly backwards and forward. Fishermen bustled inside their boats, loading them up with ropes and nets and all the clobber of their trade. A child splashed along the rim of the water, the legs of his wet trousers draping round his knees, while his mother and grandmother chorused a loud 'No!' He splashed back towards them and then into the sea again, followed joyously by the family dog.

'Would you be okay to take us over now, Guthrie?' George asked.

The man he spoke to was hauling ropes into his fishing

boat, coiling them like snakes onto the deck. They were bearded with green weeds. He glanced up at George and Ellie and looked away again, saying nothing.

'It would be nice to just sit here,' Ellie murmured. 'And paint. And what about your Aunt Izzie? Aren't we supposed to go there to wait for your dad?'

George chose not to hear her, and she didn't really expect him to. She was intrigued by his eagerness; by the way he stared out at the misty horizon as if he was trying to conjure up the shape of an island just for her. She turned away and watched the moored yachts swaying restlessly on the water, their sides rippling with the sunlight reflected off the waves. *I could paint them*, she told herself. She tried to guess the colours she would need. Dad had taught her to do that. *A titanium sea*, she thought, *with just a thin wash of the blue of the sky. The reflected masts are just squiggles, not straight at all.*

'Really calm today,' George said, coming to stand by her.

'Is it? Looks quite choppy to me, away from the shore.'

'Nah. Couldn't be better. Tide's just right, if he'll take us.'

'But he doesn't seem to want to.' She gazed at the water again, at the luminous light. How could she paint that? Almost the colour of ice really, away from the jetty. Not titanium there. Tiny ripples, and every one with a spark of sunlight on it. A man pulled away from the shore in a red rowing boat, with strong, sure strokes of his arms. Dad would put him just at the side of the painting, she thought. A kind of distraction, so it was the stretch of the sea that was the main subject.

Guthrie stood up abruptly to start up the motor on his boat and George stepped another pace towards the end of the jetty. Ellie watched him, noticing the tension in his shoulders and how he flexed his fingers anxiously at his sides.

'Can we come with you?' he called

'She's not your sister,' Guthrie muttered, without looking up.

'She's Morag's friend.'

Hardly that, Ellie thought. *We're in the same section of the city youth orchestra, if that counts as being friends. This is such a weird situation. It's so embarrassing, but I don't know how to get out of it.*

'I only like family to go there. Your father knows that well.'

'Dad's coming later, with Morag. Ellie, look!' George glanced round at her, his face lit up. He pointed to the horizon. 'That's it.'

The misty shreds of clouds that covered the horizon

shifted a little, revealing what at first was just a gloomy lump of rock; and then the sun shafted light onto the purple and emerald of a distant island. A thin white ruff of foam frothed round its base.

'Wild Island. There, it's gone again.'

'It looked . . . mysterious, what I saw of it.'

'It is.'

'I wouldn't advise the young girl to go there,' Guthrie said, still not looking at them, but at the state of his rough hands. 'Now you know, lassie. Don't go. And you're not one of the family.' He turned back to his boat.

Ellie shivered involuntarily. 'What does he mean?' she whispered.

'Take no notice of him. He's got strange ideas,' George muttered. 'But he'll take us over, if I ask him again. He can't really refuse. We don't have to wait for the others. I'll send Dad a text to tell him we've gone ahead. Let's go now! What do you think?'

Ellie looked at the distant swirl of mist and foam that was the island and shivered again. She could sense that Guthrie was watching her now, and she turned away. 'I don't know. I don't think I can.'

'I cannot wait,' Guthrie shouted. 'I have the state of the

tide in mind. Come if you must, but come now. I'm going in the next minute.'

'I know.' George's voice was tight, his face creased with misery.

'Would you go anyway?' Ellie asked him.

'How can I?' He frowned, miserable. 'Can't just leave you here, can I?'

Much as she disliked him, Ellie felt a tinge of sympathy for George. He was saddled with her against his will, he hardly knew her, and he was desperate to get to his island. Maybe she should go for just a few hours, just to please him. It touched her that he wouldn't go without her. She was nothing to do with him. *What would my mother say if I went to an island with a boy who was a virtual stranger*, she wondered. *But what would she care? My mother has other things on her mind now. And Dad? Would he care?* Dad would say, *Go! Go for the adventure. We need new experiences to feed the imagination. Treasure them. Paint them.*

'That's it. I'm casting away,' Guthrie called. 'You'll have to wait till tomorrow.'

With a groan, George stuffed his hands into his pockets and turned away. The clouds lifted from the island again, thinning to a brief shaft of misty light. *It's beautiful*, Ellie thought. *He's right.* Almost without thinking, she stepped past him to the end of the jetty. She lowered her rucksack onto the deck of the boat and jumped in after it. George laughed like a child and swung himself down beside her, and, saying nothing, shaking his head, Guthrie swung the boat away from the jetty. Ellie was elated, spray showering her, wind streaming back her hair, breath snatched. She looked across at the island; there it was again, gleaming in sunlight; and then once again it was sombre in the shadow of clouds.

That was how it happened.

Ellie could still hear the worried, repetitive bark of the splashing dog. She looked back towards Kyle. At the far end of the line of tidy white cottages stood the squat tower of the church, with its white and gold clock face. 'Twenty past three,' she murmured, as if it was of great consequence. The small shell-white beach was filled with the bustle of holiday: children falling, exploring, crying, shouting; sunshades and wind-breaks. A fat lobster-coloured man strode along the shore carrying an ice-cream cone in front of him like an Olympic torch. On the promenade behind the beach she could see a boat being hauled down a slipway and into the sea by a tractor. A yacht overturned, and the two women who had been sailing were flung overboard, screeching with laughter. One stood on the keel to try to right the dinghy, and it swung completely over and dropped her back in. Even the extraordinary was ordinary that day, fixing itself in her mind as if she already knew that this tangible, rational world was going to slip away from her into lean wisps of memory.

'There's the train we came on, going back now.' George bent towards her, lifting his voice above the throb of *Miss Tweedie*'s engine. They both watched in silence as the train wove its way, windows glinting, between the houses, and finally disappeared towards the dark mountains. *Nothing is in my control now*, Ellie thought.

'Texted your Dad?' she mouthed at George. He shook his head, saying something she couldn't interpret. He turned away then, his eyes fixed on the black rock on the distant horizon. As they drew nearer, it began to stretch itself out into a long green mound rising out of the water like a dozing sea creature.

'That's our cottage,' George mouthed at her, pointing to the creature's tiny white eye. More features became clear: inlets, gullies, caves and creeks. On the headland, as they swung round it, she saw a cliff face speckled white and black with screaming sea birds swooping round it, and perched on the point – a lighthouse.

George turned to Ellie, his face lit up with excitement, shouting something that she couldn't hear for the noise of the gulls keening round them. She loved the fact that he was sharing his pleasure with her, that he was so different from the surly George of that morning.

'A lighthouse!' she mouthed back, excited too now. 'I love lighthouses!'

The sea birds bombed towards Guthrie's boat and then swerved away as if they could see or smell that there was no fish on board, and rose up like blown pale scraps of paper into the sky. Ragged spray was flung from the rocks around the island as Guthrie nosed his boat towards the tiny apron of shore. He cut the engine and let the boat drift in, calm. George rolled up his trouser legs and jumped out, knee-deep into water.

'Tide's not running high today, I cannot get in closer,' Guthrie said. He looked at Ellie. 'If you're quite of a mind to go ashore, lassie, you'd better jump into the sea. But I say again to you, I'd rather you didn't go there.'

'Why?'

'Don't ask me why. It's a feeling I have. I know this island well. It's not a place for you.'

BERLIE DOHERTY

Ellie hesitated, made nervous by his oddly ominous words. George just tutted, impatient for her to be off the boat. She still had time. She could stay on board, maybe, get the fisherman to take her back to shore. But would he really want to do that, when he was all kitted out for his fishing expedition? She would be a nuisance to him. She already was, she could see that. And if he did take her back to Kyle, what would she do then? *After all*, she thought, *there's nothing much at stake. I'll spend a few hours on a beautiful island with a boy who prefers his music to conversation. I'll sketch the lighthouse! It will be a present for Dad, a memory of the time he took me to one. And then I'll go back. I don't even have to talk to George. He doesn't want me there anyway. That's always been clear really. He just wanted to get to his island. And so do I now. I want to be here, in spite of what Guthrie says.*

'I'll get out now,' she said. *There. I've done it.*

'You're quite sure? I trust you know what you're doing.'

No. I don't, she thought. 'Quite sure, thanks,' she said.

'Right!' George said impatiently. 'About time! Pass me the rucksacks first.' Ellie took off her sandals and shoved them into her rucksack, then handed the bags down to him. He hooked one strap of each over his shoulders, and held up his hand to help her down. She chose to ignore it, shy

42

of making physical contact with him, and levered herself off the rocking boat, splashing up to her thighs in water.

'Careful! It's slippery here!' George warned her. She tottered and lurched and finally grabbed hold of him before her feet could skid away from her completely. The shore was blue with mussel shells, piled high on high, chinking like metal as she struggled to put her sandals back on her wet feet.

Guthrie jumped out to help George push *Miss Tweedie* back into deeper water, then he swung himself up across the gunwales.

'Bye, Guthrie. Thanks!' George called.

Guthrie grunted and lay half-in and half-out of the boat so he could turn her round with one hand on the steering wheel, then he slid himself back on board. By the time Ellie had reached the top of the little blue shore, *Miss Tweedie* had puttered out of sight, out of sound. *Gone now*, she thought. *Can't change my mind.*

George passed Ellie's rucksack back to her without a word and strode ahead of her to the cottage, up a steep sandy path that had obviously been used for hundreds of years. *He must be so fed up*, she told herself. *He's lumbered himself with me for the next few hours, and he's obviously annoyed with Guthrie.*

I probably won't get a word out of him now. Without turning round, he waved his arm and pointed to a small walled enclosure, and broke into a run to reach it. Ellie sauntered along and then, realising that the enclosure actually housed the white cottage she had seen from *Miss Tweedie*, she was fired again by his excitement. By the time she caught up, George had reached the cottage and was leaning against the door with one shoulder, trying to force it open.

'Is there a key?' Ellie asked.

'Never locked,' he grunted. 'Gets jammed with the weather, that's all.'

He stood back and pressed his foot against the jamb, testing it to see where it was stuck.

Ellie sat down on her rucksack, watching him. 'Does it really belong to your family?'

'Well, sort of. We can use it whenever we want. Guthrie hasn't lived here for about thirty years, since the light was automated. And after that he just came over once a week to service the lantern.'

'What does that mean?'

The question was obviously too stupid for him to answer. He put his back to the door, tensing his feet against the ground. She wondered whether she should help him, and decided to leave it to him. It would be too embarrassing, after all, to be standing at his side grunting and pushing the way he was. 'It's not in use at all now. They moved the light out to sea years ago. A lightship. Ah – that's got it.'

'Pity the lighthouse isn't used now, though.'

'S'pose so. Never thought about it, really. We've been coming here since I was little, but I've never seen it in use. It's just there, like a great – well, Mum calls it a phallic symbol, to tell you the truth.'

Ellie felt herself blushing violently. If he noticed, George ignored her discomfiture.

'Dad's been after buying the cottage for years. It does feel like it belongs to us already, though. No-one else comes here. Anyway' – he picked up his rucksack and opened the door fully – '*Entrez.*'

The door led straight into the kitchen, which was made of corrugated iron, painted cream and blue on the inside. There was a pot sink under the window, a draining board heaped with plates, bowls, mugs and cutlery, a lamp hanging from a hook on the ceiling, a single camping gaz cooker, and a larder stacked with tins and jars. *Life is but a day at most,* the yellow chalk fading now, was written on a notice board.

'Robbie Burns,' Ellie said. 'Even I know that one.'

Another door led into the living room, which was dark

and pretty bare, with the one small window looking straight out to sea. There was a table under the window, and four wooden chairs, and a worn settee with a stunning blue blanket thrown across it, which exactly echoed the blue of the sky outside the window. The floor had stone tiles, with an old-fashioned red and black peg-rug. The fireplace was red brick, with a stone surround, and carved into it, Ellie noticed, the initials A. M.

'Who's A. M?' she asked.

'Don't know. An early lighthouse keeper, maybe. Or a miner. They had a couple of copper mines here – maybe a miner lived in the cottage for a bit. We think he did this too – we found it under the wallpaper.' He lifted a framed photograph of a vivid red sunset off the wall and revealed a blue slate with a boat carved onto it. It was almost like a child's drawing, more like half a watermelon than a rowing boat, with loopy waves under it and birds like pairs of eyebrows around it. The word *Specter* was carved beneath it.

'I like it,' Ellie said. 'It's like a primitive cave painting.'

'Pity they couldn't spell it right. Doesn't half annoy Dad, that! That's why we have to keep it covered up.' George laughed and put the sunset photograph back, slightly awry.

He's talking to me, Ellie realised. *Lots. He's human, after all.*

46

Maybe he's forgiven me for coming. Maybe he's decided to make the best of an awful situation.

'It's lovely.' Ellie gazed round. 'Really old-fashioned.'

'Yeah, you could say that! I don't think it's changed much since the first keeper lived here, way back in the early eighteen hundreds.'

There were two other doors in the little sitting room. She pushed open one of them.

'Can I look round?'

'Go ahead.'

Ellie wandered into a narrow passageway that led to two small rooms. She imagined keepers past using the cottage, moving as she was doing from room to room, raising the dust, polishing the stone flags with their feet. She went into one of the rooms, which was bare except for some hooks on the walls to hang clothes from. There was a little fireplace, painted blue. Above the mantelpiece was a framed painting of a sea scene, hung so it reflected the light from outside. A tile on the wall read *Never give all the heart. W B Yeats.* Bill Donaldson seemed to leave his mark wherever he went. There were no curtains at the window, except for the lacework of grey cobwebs. Beyond that, the blue sea gleamed. *How huge the sea is*, she thought, peering through the dusty webs. *How vast and empty and ancient and for ever it is.* And yet she could hear nothing of the sea, or the gulls outside, or of George in the other end of the cottage. The room was still, hung in a pent, listening silence.

'What do you think?' George came up so quietly behind her that she jumped, startled. 'Morag sleeps in here. Mum and Dad have the room at the back. It just looks out onto a grassy bank. This is the best room.'

'Can't they see the sea from theirs?'

'They can just see the lighthouse. Dad's set a mirror into the bank outside, so he can see the sky from his bed. He can look at the stars and the planets and the Milky Way without having to crick his neck. We've got some beds on order for these two rooms, but they haven't come yet. I use the settee usually. But we've got airbeds, when they arrive. You'll be okay here?'

'We'll be fine. Me and Morag.'

'Tonight, I mean. There's no airbed. It's still in the car.'

'Tonight?' She closed her eyes, and breathed out slowly. At last she understood. 'You mean we're not going back to Kyle?'

'How?'

'I thought Guthrie would be taking us back later.' Her

head was spinning. *Fool, fool, why didn't I think? Why didn't I ask?*

George lifted his hands in a helpless gesture. 'When could he fetch us? He won't be back from fishing till the next tide – about half past three in the morning! He'll be going straight home with his catch, not coming to the island to pick us up.'

'What about your Aunt Izzie? Won't she be expecting us?'

He shrugged. 'I doubt it will have entered Dad's head to tell her to expect us. And anyway, she wouldn't worry. Everything depends on the tides when we come here. She's used to it. We only stay with her if the tide's not right for sailing over. We either phone her from the shore or just turn up. So she wasn't expecting us in the first place.'

'Oh. Right.' She tried to sound calm, tried to hide her distress and confusion. What a family. So casual, so independent. She wasn't used to anything like this. Her life used to be so ordered and controlled, until it fell to pieces around her. How could she have been pulled along like this, just because he was so keen to get to his island? Now she was stuck with him, and he with her, and nobody actually knew they were here except Guthrie.

George suddenly seemed to realise her embarrassment.

He plugged his music back in and clattered noisily down the passage. Ellie put her hands over her face. How could she have been so stupid? Now she was aware that she could hear the sea again, pounding like the reverberations of her own pulse. She started to pull feebly at the cobwebs lacing the window, but they wound stickily round her fingers. She tugged them away and left the rest hanging, swaying like shrouds.

CHAPTER FIVE

Ellie trailed after George. He had gone outside, leaving the door wide open. She went out after him, awkward, not knowing what to do with herself now. She wandered aimlessly round the side of the cottage. The long grass was speckled with pink thrift and yellow tormentil; she knew the names from Nan. And now and again something that looked like tall overgrown cabbages, their leaves turned to lace by caterpillars. She saw George striding down a steep rubbly slope swinging a red plastic bucket from each hand. He stopped by a metal post with a levered arm and a spout, and placed one of the buckets under it. He pumped slowly, lifting his arm occasionally to brush back the flop of his hair. Eventually water began to spurt out and trickle slowly into the bucket. Futile anger rose up in her. *No running water.* She slumped down on the grass, her arms looped round her calves, head pressed into her knees. *Basic*, Sheila Donaldson had said. It was primitive. And she was trapped here. She swiped away the insects that were buzzing round her. How was she supposed to have guessed that she would be spending the night sleeping on bare floorboards in a room full of cobwebs and spiders? *Dad, Dad, come and take me home. I only came here because of you. Because you left me behind.*

George was intent on his task, jerking a tune of some sort between his teeth. Eventually he straightened up, easing his back. He took out one of his earphones and let it dangle on its cord. 'We came over in such a hurry that I didn't have time to pick up any supplies.'

'Supplies,' she repeated wearily. 'You mean food.' *God,* she thought. *He's hopeless. Hopeless.*

'That sort of thing, yes. Mum orders it from Molly Duncan's before we arrive. You know, milk, bread, matches, bottles of water. That sort of stuff.'

'So there's no food here?'

'No fresh food. There'll be tinned stuff. Dad and I were here at Easter.'

'Easter? That was in March! You must have been frozen.' She heard the rise of sarcasm in her voice, and didn't try to check it.

'It's the best time to come. Really high tides, strong winds

– excellent! Dad loves it then too. He's writing a collection of poetry, and he says there's nowhere on earth he would rather be when he's writing. Anyway' – he stopped pumping water for a moment, stared round, lifted his hands – 'we love this place.' He carried on pumping water, breathing heavily now with the effort of every stroke, till one of the buckets was full. He eased it to one side and replaced it with the empty one.

Ellie pulled at the grass, plaiting the strands intently. 'I saw a black bucket by the door. Shall I fetch it?'

'God, no. That's the loo.'

'The loo!'

'I'll put some Elsan in it later. Disgusting stuff. Smells of bananas. We have to empty it into the sea. After we've used it. When the tide's going out, of course, otherwise it gets washed back in again!' He was trying to make light of it, she knew. Maybe he recognised her anger and embarrassment. 'You get used to it,' he added brusquely. 'Here, have a go at this.' He stepped away, hooking himself back into his music. Ellie stood up and dusted herself down. She worked the pump so clumsily that water splashed all over her legs and sprayed off her onto George. He laughed, picked up the full bucket and started back to the cottage, not offering her any help. She carried on pumping, slowly, slowly, till at last she got into the rhythm of it. It felt good finally to be doing something positive. She didn't look up again until the bucket was full. Only then was she conscious that she was being watched. She straightened up, wiping her face with her forearm. George was standing some distance away, with his back to her, pretending to be staring out to sea. He turned when the pumping stopped, and stepped forward and lifted the bucket carefully.

'I'll carry it, because it's heavy.'

'We don't want to lose any.'

'Course not. And then we'll eat something.'

After all, there was no need to panic. There was actually plenty of food in the larder, and George found some matches in a jar to light the gaz cooker. They still had some of the cake and the fruit that Sheila had pushed into Ellie's bag that morning.

'Do you want me to cook something?' Ellie asked hesitantly.

'Why? I can do it. I always do the cooking here. Dad's useless.'

George prepared what he called a 'red mess' of tinned tomatoes and kidney beans and pasta, and while it was simmering on the gaz cooker Ellie took a damp cloth into the bedroom and cleaned away the cobwebs from the window, wiped the floorboards and unrolled the sleeping bag that George had found for her in a chest of rather mouldy-smelling bedding. She would use that as a mattress, and then sleep in the lightweight one that Sheila had given her. When Morag and Bill came she would have an airbed. That would be luxury. She pushed open the window and breathed in the sea, saw the sea heaving and glinting, heard the sea singing to itself.

It's beautiful, she said to herself. *I've never seen anything so beautiful.* Her anger and anxiety had all dissolved. It would be fine.

She saw that George had taken a plate of food outside and was sitting perched on a boulder, eating his red mess with a spoon. She went into the kitchen, helped herself from the pan, then instead of sitting at the table with it, decided to follow him out. She felt calmer now.

'We get some amazing sunsets here,' he said, not looking at her but at the way the rose of the sky was reflected like stained glass on the flat water.

'It's lovely.'

'It's a magical place, if you'll let it work its spell on you.'

His voice was soft, with the hush of the evening in it.

She watched him for a while, discreetly. The setting sun cast a golden light across his face and his arms, bronzing him, gilding his hair. He sensed that she was looking at him and turned to look at her and, embarrassed again, she stammered out, 'Perhaps we should phone your dad and see how Morag is.'

'Ellie . . .'

'Are you telling me there's no mobile connection?' She tried to quell the rising panic in her voice. She wouldn't even be able to contact her school friends.

'Get used to it. We're on Wild Island.'

'Your mum wanted me to send her that number,' she remembered.

'Too late.'

He stood up, the tranquillity of the moment broken. He held out his hand for her empty plate and stacked it on his own.

'I'll wash them,' she offered.

'I'll just wipe them with some kitchen paper, then we'll wash up everything properly later. We don't waste water here. Well, you saw what an interesting chore it was to get any. And we don't waste gaz, either, to boil it up. Leave them till there's a sink full, then do everything. We might want a cup of something later.' His voice trailed behind him as he set off along a sandy track away from the cottage and disappeared into a hollow.

'Right.' She bit her lip. What to do? What on earth to do now?

She climbed down the broad track that led back to the blue mussel beach where Guthrie had landed them earlier. *I could paint some shells, to show Dad*, she thought. *They're so beautiful, such an intense, strong colour, but so fragile. I can't walk on them without breaking them.* She decided she would paint them right there, where she was sitting, where the early evening sun warmed their colours so richly. *Blue, purple, indigo, violet, white, cream, yellow ochre, brown to make black*, she muttered to herself as she scrunched her way up to the cottage collect her art things. When she came back down she squatted with her knees drawn up in front of her to make a table. *Just a quick sketch*, she told herself, *or you'll get cramp.*

She would start with making some notes, as Dad had always taught her to do. 'You'll never get it exactly as you want it,' he once told her, when she had crumpled up a failed painting in exasperation and screwed it into a ball for the bin.

'Don't worry about that. Jot down a few words about what you see, and why you wanted to paint it. And never take a photograph to work from. That's a photographer's art, not a painter's. Always be aware of what's beyond the frame. Be aware of the life in your subject. Paint with your seventh sense.'

'Seventh?' she had laughed. 'What's that?'

'You'll know. One day, when you get it right, you'll know.'

Dad, she scribbled. *If I was taking a photograph I would fill the frame with the shells just as they are around me, so you got a sense of the thousands of them, piles and layers of them. But I'll paint just one, perhaps, with just a blur of colour wash behind it. Do that ay, then draw my shell. I love its darkness, almost black at the nub, and the richness of the purple, and the purity of the white where its skirt flares out. The colours just drain into each other. It's a bit like an iris, maybe?*

'Time of day,' she imagined him saying.

Early evening. About six or seven? Lovely, golden light across the mussel beach.

She stopped writing and concentrated on drawing the perfect shape of the shell, and then in mixing her paints to get exactly the right sequence and merging of colours. She was aware of someone moving behind her, peering over her shoulder. Instinctively she covered up the painting with her hand. She hated to have anyone watching while she was drawing or painting, unless it was Dad. 'Just doing a quick picture for my dad,' she muttered, and then glanced reluctantly over her shoulder. George had gone. *He's as quick as a cat*, she thought. *And how rude of him to look at my painting and say nothing. He probably thought it was awful.* She packed away her paint things. She wasn't satisfied with her picture, after all. The colours were too elusive. *Useless, Dad. It's rubbish.*

As she went up to the cottage she saw George approaching from the other direction. How odd. He must have moved really quickly, pretending he hadn't been at the shell beach at all. How strange he was. He was carrying driftwood in his arms, and Ellie followed as he went straight into the cottage with it and scattered it across the hearth.

Ellie knelt down to look at the pieces.

'Lovely shapes,' she said.

'Sometimes they just look like animals, or birds. There's a really nice one that we've left on one of the beaches, where we found it. It just looks right there. We pulled it up above high tide line so it doesn't get washed away again.'

'You'll have to show me.'

'You'll have to find it.'

'Oh. Right.'

'It's better that way. Been painting something?'

'It didn't work.'

'Can I see?'

She shook her head. He'd seen enough, surely. He knew how poor it was.

'You know it didn't. You saw it,' she said defiantly. 'Down there. You were watching me.'

He laughed. 'Why should I watch you? You're as bad as Mum. She's always saying she's being watched, especially when she's on her own down there. It's rubbish.'

'But you *were* there, weren't you?'

He laughed and went outside, wiping his hands on his T-shirt, then paused and looked back at her. 'It'll be dark soon, so I'm going to Landlook Point. You can come with me, if you don't want to be here on your own.'

Is he mocking me, she wondered? But he was right. She felt oddly uneasy now. She didn't want to be on her own in the cottage. 'Okay.' She shrugged carelessly. 'Is it far?'

'Nothing's far. About ten minutes at my speed. But, actually, you just get used to sauntering when you're on the island. There's never any rush here.'

Without waiting for her he headed away from the cottage on a well-worn sandy path through the grass. Hands in pockets, head down, striding, he seemed to have completely forgotten about her. She followed him slowly, determined not to run after him like a pet dog or something. If this was what he called sauntering, she couldn't imagine what he would do when he was in a hurry. The path petered out into little more than a rabbit track, down onto crinkled shell-sand and a rocky outcrop. Here he was waiting for her. He held out a hand to help her over the slippery boulders, and she felt herself blushing. She pretended she hadn't noticed him. All the same, she was aware of his closeness to her, balanced as they were, side by side on a single flat slab of rock.

'There's no sea here now,' said Ellie. 'Just wet sand.'

'It's low tide at the moment. Just about as low as it gets before the tide turns and it starts to build up again. Do you know about the tides?'

'Sort of. Governed by the moon.'

'Right. It's the magnetic pull of the moon that causes them. When the tide turns, it will be flood tide; it gradually starts to build up and flood towards land.'

'Then it's high tide. Like it was when we arrived.'

'And when it's turned again, it's called ebb tide, till it

reaches this low point again.' He glanced at her. 'Here endeth the lesson,' he grinned. 'This is when the waders come. See the curlews, dipping their long beaks into the mud? And the little black and white birds with orange beaks? They're oystercatchers. They both have really sweet calls.'

'Not like those screechy gulls.' She giggled, nervous because he was so close to her; so gentle with his voice just now. They listened to the piping call of the oystercatchers, not moving, not speaking. She could hear the draining of the sea into the sand; the ruffle of the soft breeze against the rocks.

'Kyle looks tiny from here,' George murmured. 'Just a cluster of white cottages and a thin strip of beach.'

'It's so still. It's so very still now. And the sky is so pale, there's hardly any colour left in it.'

They both fell silent again, aware of each other, aware of the twilight and the first stars.

'See that sandbank – between here and the mainland?' George said suddenly. 'It's completely exposed at the moment. Can you see it?'

'It looks as if we could walk across to it.'

'You can't though. It's a trick of the light. When the tide's ebbing you see a wrack of heaped-up sand and cockleshells just showing up out of the water like a pathway, as if it's leading right to the sandbank. It's caused by the way the tide sweeps round both sides of the island like a horseshoe, and smashes into itself at the other side. Probably at one time, centuries ago maybe, the wrack was completely exposed. But you can't cross to the sandbank on it now. It's surrounded by a moat of water, always. Never, never be tempted to walk out to the sandbank.'

'Why would I?' Ellie laughed, trying to ease away the unbidden alarm she felt at his sudden seriousness.

'You have been warned.' He put on a voice like an automaton and laughed easily with her. 'But I'm serious – there's sinking sand, for a start, and that moat around it is full of treacherous currents, and all kinds of gullies snaking round, like rivers. They're all filled up with sinking sand now. It looks solid, but it isn't. And when the tide comes in it rushes down these gullies. It's fascinating, the way the tide changes; the power the water has, the way the gullies and creeks fill up and coves just disappear.'

He was so animated now. He was so much nicer when he talked to her like this. She found herself smiling as she watched him.

'Ellie, people have drowned, trying to cross from the

mainland, thinking they could walk to Wild Island. Dad warns me about it every time I come here. Never, never even try.'

He stayed still, his eyes fixed on the mainland, and then said, 'Watch the town. Kyle. Watch the streetlamps coming on, twinkling across the wet sand. I love to see that.'

She looked out across to the green embrace of the mainland, darkening steadily as the light began to fall.

'I think I can make out the church. It's so tiny, though. I wonder what they're all doing – all those people we left behind on the shore? It's as if they don't exist any more.'

'There!' he interrupted her. 'Look! Can you see a light flashing right at the end of town – where you said the church is?'

'Oh yes.'

'It's Aunt Izzie!' George laughed. 'That's what we do when we come to the island – every night at about this time we flash our torches to each other to say goodnight! So. She knows we're here, then. Dad must have phoned her after all.'

'Sounds like something out of *Swallows and Amazons*.' Ellie giggled.

'Probably is. Dad and Izzie were born in that house, and they used to come over here lots when they were kids. Years

64

ago. They probably did proper semaphore then. I tried to learn it once, but I can never remember it. Oh, she's flashing it again! And again. Okay, Izzie, we got the message.'

'Are we supposed to flash back?'

'We would if we had torches. But guess what?'

'They're in the car.'

'Dad'll bring them tomorrow. There is one here but the battery's flat. We need to get wind-ups, but they wouldn't be powerful enough for that distance anyway. He'll bring everything we need.'

No torch. No electricity. No bathroom. No mobile signal. Nothing. Ellie thought. *Dad. Do you hear that? Nothing.*

'Another thing,' George said. 'You see those rocks just below us? Flat topped, leading out into the sea?'

'I do. They're like stepping stones.'

'Exactly. It looks as if you could wade straight in from that last one, into shallow water. Don't do it! It's very deep there. They're called Lone Lassie's stones.'

Ellie laughed again. 'Who was the Lone Lassie?'

He shrugged. 'No idea. These names hang on through time, don't they? Pieces of lost history.'

'Only the stones remember.'

'Perhaps you're right. Shall we go back?'

They turned away from the distant twinkling lights of the mainland. The stars were growing brighter now, huge and plentiful; they seemed to bloom out of the darkening sky like flowers unfolding. They walked in silence, conscious of each other, and of the warm air soft on them, and the gentle scuff of their feet on the grass.

'Do you want a cup of anything? Well, there's only tea, actually,' George offered as they reached the door. They were standing in darkness.

'I think I'll go straight to bed,' Ellie said, awkward again. There was the dreadful black bucket by the door. How awful, how embarrassing everything was. And would she clean her teeth at the kitchen sink? George lit the only candle, stuffed his earphones back in and turned away from her with a casual lift of his hand. Perhaps he was as embarrassed as she was. Perhaps he too had been aware of that tender silence as they had walked back together and, like Ellie, had been half afraid of it.

Ellie went down the passage slowly, her rucksack draped over her shoulder. She groped in the dimness of the room for her night things, and found her sleeping bag. She slid inside it, aware of the rustling sound she was making, softly aware of the similar rustling sounds of George in the living room down the corridor. Her mind drifted over the strange events of the day. Maybe, after all, she had made the right decision. Tomorrow, Morag and Bill would come. Things would be better then. Maybe.

She closed her eyes and lay listening for a long time to the hushed, soothing sigh of the sea; and at last, imperceptibly, drifted into a deep sleep.

CHAPTER SIX

She was awakened suddenly by an ice-cold kiss on her cheek. She started, instantly alert, wide-eyed and shocked, listening to a movement in her room that was as stealthy as the sifting of sand. She raised herself on one elbow, peering into furls of darkness.

'Is that you?' she whispered. She could hear the shake of fear in her voice.

Nothing. She lowered herself down, breathing deeply to try and calm herself.

Yet there it came again; a scarcely perceptible rustling. Perhaps Bill and Morag had come on the early tide, that could be it, she thought. Perhaps Morag was feeling her way about the room, trying not to disturb her.

'Who is it?' she called again, louder this time. 'It's okay. I'm awake. Morag. I can hear you.' She was frightened now by the total, deafening silence around the quaver of her voice. 'Who is it?' Her nails were biting into the palm of her hand.

Now she heard the quick tread of someone running along the passage. She was aware of the darker than darkness bulk of a tall figure in the doorway.

'Are you okay?' George asked.

'I thought I heard someone in the room. I thought it was Morag.'

'She's not here.'

'Was it you?'

'Not me.'

'Over there. By my rucksack.'

Their muted voices tossed in the blackness like an invisible ball passing to and fro. Throw. Catch. Throw. Listen.

'Do you know what?' George said at last. 'It's mice.'

'*Mice!*'

'I'm sorry. I should have warned you. They're all over the place at night. Dad'll fix something up tomorrow.'

'Mice! I don't believe it.' She sank back, gulping in draughts of air, trying to calm herself.

'You're not scared of them, are you?'

'I've never seen a mouse,' she muttered. 'Not a real one. Not in our house.'

'Only mice. They're so tiny. Let's face it, this is their house, really.'

She could sense the darkness that was George lowering himself, sliding down to sit on the floor, leaning his back against the wall. 'For ninety per cent of the time they have the house all to themselves. We just don't leave food around, don't encourage them. Most of the time we just get on with them.'

'I see.'

'Only mice,' he repeated. He stayed, listening with her, trying to reassure her maybe that there was nothing there to harm her. It was comforting to know he was there, after all. Ellie closed her eyes, listening to the quiet sound of his breathing on the other side of the room.

'You could go to Dad's room, if you like. Won't be much different. Or swap with me.'

'I might. I'll see how I get on. It's not so bad, now I know what it is.' *Now you're here*, she might have said, but daren't.

'About your dad,' he said after a pause. 'That was a terrible mistake before. I feel really bad about that.'

'It wasn't your fault,' she replied to the darkness. 'Don't worry about it.'

'Cornwall! Apparently it's a great place. You can get there

70

yourself – there's a train that goes all the way to Penzance. It takes all day, but you'd get there.'

'I know.'

'And there's Skype. Have you tried that?'

Silence again, and into it, surreptitiously, the creep of mouse scrabblings.

'Now I know what it is, I'm not so scared. Quite.'

'Why did he go to Cornwall? Your dad? You don't have to tell me . . .'

Ellie raised herself back up on one elbow. It was easier to talk like this, to a voice in the darkness. 'Mum threw him out last Christmas and started going with someone else. Angus, he's called. I call him Sweatyhead. Dad stayed near town, so I still saw a lot of him. Some evenings after school and every weekend, it was me and Dad. But last week he went to live in England, and yesterday—' She paused. Was it really only yesterday? 'On Saturday, she married Angus. She hardly even knows him! I hate him. I hate her.' She had never said as much as this to anyone. Not even Hannah. She had never found a voice for it.

'Don't. You've only got one mum.'

He stood up. She could hear him creaking along the passage again.

'And I hate the mice,' she said.

'That's tough.'

'I don't like the idea of them running over my face in the dark.'

She could hear George laughing. He was back in the little sitting room, sliding himself into his sleeping bag, laughing. 'Neither do I,' he called. 'Good night, Ellie.'

I hate him too, she thought.

CHAPTER SEVEN

The next morning it was as if they had never had that conversation. When Ellie went downstairs, she found an opened tin of prunes and an opened tin of rice pudding on the table, with a bowl and spoon alongside them. She shuddered slightly at the thought of eating stuff like that for breakfast. But there was no bread, no cereals, no fruit juice. She used some of the pumped-up water to wash her face at the kitchen sink, and discreetly watched George through the kitchen window. He was outside on his boulder, eating his breakfast and reading at the same time. It looked like a new book. She squinted at the title, trying to make it out from where she was standing. *Wild Places*. He looked completely at ease with himself. Ellie spooned a little out of the tins into a bowl, poured the rest into two other bowls and covered them with plates against the mice. She was too shy to join him this time, but ate her strange breakfast at the table. She found herself staring at the words on the empty tins, as if they had important messages for her concealed in the lists of ingredients.

George wandered in with his bowl and wiped it clean with a piece of damp kitchen roll.

'You found it, then.'

'It's a weird breakfast,' Ellie said.

'Dad'll bring cereals and stuff, and milk. I told you.'

'I wasn't complaining.'

He started rummaging in the chest that had contained the bed things and brought out a creased towel. He stood up with it draped round his neck, watching her thoughtfully.

'I'm going for a swim.'

'Fine.'

'Want to come?'

'No. It's okay.'

'Fine.'

'Where do I put the empty tins?'

He turned back, fished a roll of bin bags out of the chest, and handed one to her. 'Don't leave it lying round,' he warned.

'Because of the mice.'

'We put all the rubbish in that box round the back, and then it goes home with us.' He hesitated. 'In that chest thing you'll find an old cozzie of Morag's from when she was about twelve. It'll probably fit you, you're so . . .'

Skinny. Go on, say it. 'I'm not really keen on swimming.'

'Okay. It's there, if you change your mind.' He paused, watching her again, as if he wanted to say something else and couldn't find the words. And suddenly it was obvious to Ellie that he did want her to go with him. He wanted to show her the island. He wanted to share it with her. And, after all, she had sort of lied about the swimming. She knelt down by the chest and took out the costume. It would be too small, even for her.

'I'm just a bit nervous about swimming in the sea. I've never done it before.'

'There's a safe creek that opens into a lagoon. That's where we swim.'

'Right.'

'It's near a smugglers' cave.'

'Of course. You couldn't have an island without smugglers.' *Oh, why did I say that,* she thought, *I sound so scornful.* She didn't mean it to be.

'It's true though. Have a look yourself at low tide. The whole shape of the island changes then – you see rocks that have been lurking under the water all the time waiting to tear the bottom out of boats. Caves and creeks and shores appear, like mouths opening up. The island you know changes into an island you don't. The weather changes it too, the sun and the wind and the rain all turn it into something different.' His fingers danced as he talked, animated. 'Wait till you see the smugglers' cave. You could easily hide a boat in there. It's even got a rock shelf where they would have hauled up their contraband. Anyway' – he turned away – 'it's near where we swim. It's very safe. I'll show you where the lagoon is, and you can just go there any time.'

'Okay.' She shrugged. 'I'll just come and see it.'

She pushed her empty bowl away and stood up to follow him out of the cottage, hesitating just for a moment by the clothes chest, then deciding against opening it to look for a towel. She was too shy to swim with him, anyway. It would be too intimate. She was surprised to find that he was still waiting for her this time. He was sitting on the wall outside the cottage, humming to himself. He glanced across at her when she came out, then raked his fingers self-consciously through the floppy drape of his hair over his eyes. They said nothing as they walked. Their silence was clumsy with unspoken questions. Yet it was a perfect day, the gulls laughing, the sea silver with sunlight. *How do I paint that, Dad?* she wondered. *That light on the sea is so bright. Could you do a painting that was so bright that people had to screw up their eyes to look at it, like I'm doing now?*

George started singing quietly to himself again, breaking the silence.

'You're not wearing your earphones.'

'Battery's flat.'

'Ah. And you can't charge it.' *That means we'll have to talk to each other*, she thought. *Panic.* 'What kind of music do you like?'

'Not the sort you and Morag play. Nothing with strings. Got to have words. You know, deep, meaningful stuff.' He had shifted his voice into a self-mocking tone, then laughed. 'Can't stand strings.'

She giggled. 'I'm not that keen on that stuff either. I'm not very good at music anyway. I like dancing though. That's my favourite thing to do.'

'I can tell,' he said. 'You move like a dancer.'

'Do I?' She blushed quickly and glanced away. *I can't believe he noticed*, she thought. *I can't believe he said that.* 'Mum makes me go to orchestra because she's musical herself. I quite like it, actually, I do enjoy it really, but I'm not much good. I never practise, that's the trouble. Morag's really good, though.'

'That's what I mean. She practises for hours on end. Drives me round the bend. What with her practising and Mum talking all the time and Dad reciting poetry – what can I do? I need my headphones!'

Ellie laughed again, easily this time.

'Anyway, I'm leaving home soon. Uni in October.'

'What will you do?'

'Marine biology.'

'Oh yes.' She remembered now. 'You're going to Newcastle. Morag told me. My grandparents used to live there.'

'How about you?'

'I've got another year at school yet.' She hesitated. 'And then I wanted to go to Art College. But I'm not so sure now.'

'Why?'

'I've kind of stopped painting. It's not the same now' – she paused again – 'without Dad. Mum thinks I should do something more academic anyway. She'd like me to apply to uni. She says I'll paint anyway, so why go to college to do it.'

'And what does your dad think?'

'He sort of agrees with her. He says that Art School is too prescriptive and doesn't allow you to find your own style. He says you become a painter by painting. But he doesn't realise – he's taught me everything. He shows me what to do, and how to do it, and we talk about it all the time. I can't do it without him.' Her voice trailed away. *There you are, Dad. See what you've done? I need you.*

George stepped ahead of her as if her sudden openness was embarrassing to him. He ran ahead with long loping strides down a grassy slope towards a creek. 'You have to be careful you don't tumble into this in the dark,' he called. 'It's well hidden till you get to this point.'

'I'm not likely to wander about in the dark. It's full of traps, this place. Quicksand, currents, mice, hidden creeks.'

'Oh, there's worse than that. Look, this is where we moor *Sprite*.' He pointed to a dinghy moored in the creek below them. 'We might go for a sail in her later.'

'Out on the sea, you mean?' She eyed the little green boat doubtfully and folded her arms round herself. *No, I don't fancy that*, she thought. *Trusting myself to Guthrie's bouncy old fishing boat was bad enough, but this thing looks like a floating peapod. It would capsize as soon as it felt the tumble of the waves.* 'I'm not sure.'

Did he tut? She felt he might have done.

'The thing is, the best thing, the very best thing here,

is something you can only really appreciate by boat. I was just going to row her, not sail her, just down this end of the island a bit. A few minutes.' He waited, not watching her but eyeing his green boat lovingly. 'Actually, I think I'll go anyway.'

He stepped easily into the boat and picked up the oars that were lying in the bottom. 'Completely versatile. You can row her, sail her, or use an outboard motor.'

'Okay,' she said, not wanting to be left behind, stupidly waiting for him. 'I'll come.'

He just grunted, paused briefly for her to step in, and pulled away from the bank. She clutched the gunwales as *Sprite* rocked into the central channel.

'Shouldn't we be wearing lifejackets?' she asked nervously.

'Yeah, we should really. We've got some buoyancy aids, but they're back in the house.' He carried on rowing, pulling easily out of the creek and into the sea. 'Three minutes and we'll be there.'

She clung onto the sides, watching the scrabble of water around the boat, careful to keep her eyes away from George, who was facing her as he rowed. *This is stupid*, she thought. *Dangerous and stupid. Why can't I have a mind of my own sometimes? Why didn't I just say no?*

She knew he was watching her, smiling. In spite of herself, she began to feel exhilarated. She loved the slapping sound of the waves flocking around the boat, the cool spattering of spray on her face. She trailed her hand over the edge, fingering the water.

Very soon George glanced over his shoulder and steered *Sprite* into the mouth of a sea cave. The entrance was not much wider than the boat, but as soon as they were inside the cave opened out like a church. The roof rose high over their heads, with a smaller cliff cave like a window throwing light down from about thirty feet above them. The whole cavern was filled with a glorious emerald-green light; on the water, on the walls, reflected in ripples on the roof. Rock doves purred, pale shapes on the shelves of the walls. George allowed the boat to drift round so Ellie could gaze up in awe at it all, then he dipped the oars soundlessly into the water and rowed deeper into the cave, into darkness. 'We're in the belly of the island,' he whispered. His voice pittered round them. For a moment they sat in the near darkness, with the boat swaying soundlessly, rocking them. The waves licked the sides like the lapping tongues of cats.

George swung the boat round and rowed out through the ethereal green towards the gleam that was the cave mouth, and they burst out into the full glaring blue light of day. Ellie realised that she had been holding her breath the whole time.

'Amazing,' she said. 'I've never seen anything like it. So beautiful. So peaceful.'

He dipped his head in a kind of bow.

When they reached the creek, he fastened *Sprite* to its boulder and left Ellie to climb out as best as she could. He strode away from her alongside the creek until it widened to form a perfect lagoon, as still and calm as mirror.

'See?' he called. 'This is where we swim. Quite safe!' His voice boomed around the rocks.

'It looks fine,' she agreed. 'Maybe I'll paddle.'

This time he did tut. He pulled off his T-shirt and dived in, still wearing his shorts. He disappeared completely, for several alarming seconds, then bobbed up again at the far side, lifting his arms so water dripped silver from him. Now, as Ellie watched him quartering the lagoon with his long, languid, powerful strokes, she felt a deep desire to plunge in and join him. She was shy about swimming with him, here in the emptiness of the lagoon. But she was actually a very strong swimmer. The water was so still, so smooth and inviting. She couldn't resist the urge any longer. It was as if invisible arms were linking into her own, an invisible voice coaxing her to follow George. Without thinking what she was doing, Ellie shook off her sandals and shorts and simply slid into the water, into its cool silkiness. She crossed the lagoon swiftly, head under, eyes open so she could see the clear water and blue shells below her, then she lay on her back, just floating, watching the specks of clouds and the gulls cruising above her head. *It's as if they're swimming in water and I'm drifting in sky*, she thought. She closed her eyes, rocking with just the slightest flip of her feet to keep herself afloat. *It's all right. I'm going to be all right here. I've come to the right place.*

But when she opened her eyes again, she felt suddenly cold and alone. The cliffs seemed to hang over her, echoing with soft whisperings. It was just the sound of the water she had disturbed lapping against the rocks, she told herself. A cloud passed over the sun; the air grew chill around her. Someone was watching her. She turned over, and saw that George had gone. He had taken his T-shirt with him. His unused towel was still rolled up on the rock; for her, she knew. The lagoon was deserted, and yet all around her the empty air thrummed.

CHAPTER EIGHT

They ate their lunch of leftover red mess in silence, both of them still wearing the wet clothes they had been swimming in.

'I loved that cave,' Ellie said at last.

'Good. I knew you would.'

'Is that the smugglers' cave you told me about?'

'Yeah. When I was younger, I wanted to be a smuggler when I grew up. I thought I'd live in that cave and eat fish.'

'What would you smuggle?'

'Rum, of course. Barrels and barrels of it. I didn't know what it was, though. I was going to build myself a lugger out of driftwood.'

'I'm glad you took me to see it.' She felt shy, saying that. She knew it had been a kind of present to her, and she was annoyed with herself for having nearly rejected it. She must seem an awfully timid person to him.

'You can work your way round to it on foot at very low tide, but it's not easy. You have to scramble over rocks, and they're slippery with seaweed. The best way to see it is by boat, like we did. And actually we could have beached it in there, and climbed right up inside it to that window cave. We can do that another time. With Morag. If you like.'

She noticed that he was restless; he kept glancing away from the cottage as if he was watching or listening out for something. She wondered if he was annoyed by her company, and still regretting with every minute that he had ever had the idea of bringing her to the island without Morag.

'They'll be here soon, won't they?'

He shrugged. 'Not yet. Couple of hours maybe.'

'You like being on your own. If it was just you here, you'd love it.'

'Dad used to call me the solitary mister.'

'Oh?'

'From Dylan Thomas. Welsh poet.'

'Oh.'

She took their plates indoors and decided to wash everything up, heated some water, and stood at the sink staring out while she was waiting for the water to boil on the gaz cooker. George took the emptied red bucket to the pump. She thought about Mum and Dad, the way things used to be before they fell out with one another, when they each had household jobs to get on with and just did them, moving from task to task around the house and garden like dancers intent on their own steps.

The kitchen door opened inwards, and as she stood there she realised that the window in it acted as a kind of mirror, capturing the outside from a different angle. When she lost sight of George from the window over the sink, she could just turn her head and see him reflected in the door window. She would be able to watch him coming back, staggering up the slope with the pail. The thought pleased her; the secretiveness of it. Before long she did glimpse a reflection; a quick movement, like the flicker of sun through leaves, hardly there. *There he is!* She turned to properly look at the door window – and the reflection had gone. The slope was empty.

I mustn't stay in here on my own again, she thought. *This house is unnerving me.*

And then it came again, seconds later, an action replay; the same motion, the same reflection, and unmistakeably George. He must have stopped. He must have gone back for something. She left the washing-up and went out hastily to meet him.

'I'd like to go out again, see a bit more of the island,' she said. 'Want to show me round?'

He set the pail down, amused by her childlike eagerness. 'Okay.'

'Can we get into the lighthouse?'

'Course we can. It used to be locked up, but the bolt rusted years ago.'

'Can we get right up to the lantern room?'

'Yes. They've taken the lantern away, though. It's just an empty tower. There's a really old lantern at the back of one of the sheds – a proper lantern, but that would have been used years before Guthrie came here.'

'An old paraffin lamp, you mean?'

He shrugged. 'Probably. I haven't really looked at it, to tell the truth. But I've been in the lighthouse a few times. You can get out onto the gallery, the balcony bit right up at the top. You can see for miles from there.'

'I'd like to do that.'

'Fine. But why don't you save that for later? Dad will take you up when he comes. He'd love to tell you about how lighthouses work and everything.'

She didn't tell him that her own father had taken her to a working lighthouse, not long ago. It had been one of their last trips together. 'He'll probably recite the poem about the abandoned lighthouse to me.'

'*Flannan Isle*. You're probably right. I'm afraid I know the whole thing by heart, he recites it so often.

'"Though three men dwell on Flannan Isle

To keep the lamp alight

As we steered under the lee we caught—"'

'"No glimmer through the night."' Ellie put in. 'We did it at school.'

'Right. I can't impress you with that then.'

Oh. Is that what he's trying to do? Impress me? But she saw that he was smiling; mocking himself.

'". . . So ghastly in the cold sunlight

It seem'd, that we were struck the while

With wonder all too dread for words . . ."' he went on, making his voice tremble.

'Don't,' she laughed. 'I'll never dare go in it now!'

You must. The words danced into her head as if she had heard them, as if they had been spoken aloud.

She breathed in sharply. 'But I must.'

'You will. I'd like to show you something else, before the

88

others come. Something special. My favourite place.'

'Even better than the smugglers' cave?' Maybe he really did want to please her. She smiled at him gratefully.

'Hmm. Could be. It's a close contest.'

She smiled. 'Okay.'

This is getting better, she thought. *I quite like him again now.*

'It's the other side of the Height. That's the quick way to it, but it's a bit steep.'

He put his head to one side, questioning, and she nodded. Soon, soon, it wouldn't be just the two of them any more. She would have two more relative strangers to get used to. He might retreat then into his silences, shutting her out again. Now, he chatted quite easily to her as they walked, as if they had known each other for much longer than just one strange day.

'An exiled king lived here once, on the Height,' he told her. 'Hundreds of years ago, mind. It had a castle, according to the map of the island.'

'Must have been pretty small.'

'It was probably a shed. He'd fallen out with one of the Henrys. Beware of rabbit holes, by the way. There's hundreds of rabbits on the island, and you could sprain your ankle easily.'

Ellie paused to catch her breath. Bees bumbled in and out of the heather bells, and all round her, on every side, the endless sea glinted.

'It's really lovely,' she said, and realised she was talking to herself. *He can't keep still for a minute*, she thought. She loped after George, stumbling a little as clumps of low-growing gorse and heather snagged at her ankles, following him up to the north end of the island and along the bumpy ridge towards the lighthouse. He was waiting for her there.

'It's just round the other side of the lighthouse. The very edge of the cliff, so be careful. Guthrie said a keeper once lost his way in the fog, and went over the edge. Another of the dangers of this place.'

'I'm taking my life in my hands,' she agreed, trying to hide her mounting alarm. Everything about the island was dangerous, it seemed. Beautiful and dangerous.

'Just follow me. It's fine.' He took her round the front of the lighthouse towards the edge of the cliff and the long, immeasurable sheen of the sea, and there she suddenly became aware of the unearthly heckling and reek of thousands of sea birds.

'It stinks!' she laughed.

'Luckily we can't smell or hear this anywhere else on the

island. This is the only safe place to see the cliff face, apart from in a boat. Take care because of this groin in the cliff. It's a keyhole cove, just funnelling the sea. *Ye cud plunge tae yeer deeth!*' he said dramatically. 'And you're only seeing a tiny part of it, mind. Best lie on your stomach to see it, if you get dizzy at all.'

He lay down, and she did the same, so their heads were inches from the cliff edge. They propped themselves up on their elbows and watched the sea birds clamouring around the groin of the cliff, the endless swoop and circle of them.

'What are they?'

'Mostly cormorants. Hundreds and hundreds of cormorants.'

'They look like black crucifixes.'

'Aye, when they're hanging out their wings like that to dry, they do.'

'They're a bit spooky.' She started to pull herself back, uneasy. 'I don't like them.'

He turned his head to look at her. 'Do you think so? But they're beautiful to me.' It was almost as if she had hurt his feelings. He was showing her his bird cliff as another kind of friendship present, and here she was, seemingly rejecting it again. She eased herself back down, next to him.

'What are the other ones?'

'Fulmar, kittiwake, gannets, mostly. We're lucky they're still here. They live out at sea, and they only come into land to nest. Some of them still have fledglings, that's why they're still here. See, those grey bundles on the ledges? They're the babies. They'll soon be flying. Now – watch that one coming in. Straight to its ledge, huh? Watch what it does.'

Ellie watched as the huge bird landed clumsily on the tiny ledge, and then faced its mate. Both birds spread out their wings and seemed to fence with their long beaks, clashing one against the other, and then swept their heads downwards, one neck over another, weaving round and round and calling out loudly at the same time.

'It's a tender thing to watch isn't it, in such big clumsy birds?'

'It is,' she whispered, smiling.

'They do that every time they meet. And sometimes he brings her a present.'

'Like a tasty fish.'

'Oh, or a bit of seaweed or a feather, anything he's happened to see that he thinks she'll like.'

'I bet she really wants a box of chocolates! A reward for

standing on that windy shelf for so long. They're amazing. And huge.'

'About a metre long. And each wing would be about the same. We'll bring the binoculars next time, so you can see them up close. They're really beautiful. Pale apricot heads, and icy blue eyes. You'll love them, when you see them properly. You'll want to paint them. Even the cormorants, you'll love them too. They have a beautiful iridescent sheen to them.'

'I'd like to see them more closely.'

'Dad takes the binos home every time. There's some old ones around somewhere, but they're not very powerful. Oh, look – see that gannet there, the one pointing its beak up, right up to the sky?'

'Yes. Yes, I do,' she said, catching his excitement.

'That means he's about to take off. Watch him!'

'Wow! Those huge wings! But its legs look so comical! The way it's lifting its feet up!' Ellie laughed.

'They're all a bit clumsy. Not land birds at all, you see. They're out of their element. I hope you get to see the gannets diving. They're like arrows. That's the most amazing thing in the world. We'll come and watch.'

'I'd like that.'

He shimmied himself backwards and knelt up. 'Take it slowly,' he warned her. 'You get dizzy, looking over the edge like that. Come right back, and kneel up first.'

She did as he said, and he bent down and put a hand gently under her elbow to help her up. 'Thanks,' she said. 'That was brilliant!'

'The island spell is working?'

'Oh, it is! I could watch them for hours. You'll have to tell me all the names.'

'I will. I'd like to. Now, here's one for you, this one in front of us with the deep voice. He's a great black-backed gull.'

'Great back blacked gull,' she giggled. 'Black blacked. Can't say it! Great black-backed gull! Got it!'

He touched her arm casually. 'Look at the way the waves are streaming. Scallywagging against the rocks. The tide's turned.'

'Scallywagging. I like that.' Ellie smiled. 'I can just imagine the fish down there, wagging their scallies!'

George laughed again. He shook his head as if he had met his match in Ellie. 'Good one!'

The tide has *turned*, she thought, hugging herself. *He's different. We're different.*

'It's time to go,' he said. 'The others will be here soon. We'll go to Landlook Point to watch them coming.'

He turned away, and she felt a quick pang of remorse. *It would be lovely*, she thought, *to have a few more hours, just the two of them, before Bill and Morag come.* She wondered whether George was thinking the same thing. But then, without waiting for her to catch up, he set off with his long strides for the very opposite end of the island. It was almost as if he'd forgotten all about her; had tossed the moment away so it blew with the gannets across the open sea. And the sun was turning colder, the wind was biting now, and the cliff was a dangerous place to be. She hurried after him.

When Ellie arrived at the Point, George was standing with his hands screwed into funnels over his eyes, like binoculars. 'I can see Guthrie's boat coming over,' he said. 'The blue one, see? That's *Miss Tweedie*. Should be here in about half an hour. Supplies are on their way! Hope they bring some beer.' He climbed back from the rocks and stretched himself on the grass, humming one of his made-up tunes, his hands behind his head.

'It must have been like this all the time, when the lighthouse keeper lived on the island. Watching out for the supplies.'

'I think they had plenty to do, most of the time.'

'What happened in the winter, and stormy weather? They must have been stuck here for days. Weeks, without seeing anyone.'

'They grew a few veg, and there were milk cows and hens. And they'd have fished. They'd support themselves mostly.'

'Still, it must have been lonely, even if they had families.'

'Dad said that most other lighthouses had three men – always the principle keeper and two assistants. It wasn't like their home. They moved on after every few weeks to different lights.'

'Why?'

'To stop them going mad, probably.' He turned lazily and sat up to look through his screwed up hands again. Then he scrambled to his feet. 'What's going on?'

'What's happened?'

'Guthrie's not heading for the island. He's going straight out to sea! I don't believe it. He's heading straight past us. They haven't come.'

CHAPTER NINE

George broke into a run, heading back round to the east side of the island, and Ellie realised at once where he was going. By the time she reached the creek where his little boat was moored he had already untied *Sprite* and was raising the sail.

'There's just a chance that they arrived in Kyle too late to come out with Guthrie. That's another of Dad's sayings – *Time, tide and Guthrie wait for no man*. I can bring them over in *Sprite*.'

'What if they're not there yet?'

'At least I'll be able to phone Dad from Kyle, see what's happening. Get their ETA etc.' He was excited, she could tell. She watched him tautening ropes so the red mainsail flapped lazily when he hauled it up. 'It'll be fine once we're out of the creek,' he told her. 'Lovely fresh wind for sailing. *Sprite* will love it.' He looked up at her, his eyes glinting with pleasure. 'Okay. Hop in.'

'I'd like to stay here and paint.'

He was disappointed in her, she knew. She was disappointed in herself. She had spoilt that easy, warm companionship. Yet she was unaccountably shy again. It would be better for him to arrive on his own to collect his father and Morag. They weren't together, not an item. 'Besides, there might not be room for us all. You won't be long, will you?'

'Can't be.' He was already moving away from the bank, easing *Sprite* into the centre of the creek where the water was at its highest. 'Have to come back with the tide. But I'll have time to wait an hour or so for Dad and Morag, if I find they're close to Kyle. They might have got held up by traffic, or maybe Dad hasn't checked the tide times.'

'Get some supplies?'

'Of course. Dad will have picked them up already, if he's there. What's essential? Eggs, milk, cheese, fruit, veg. Anything else? Mum will have phoned an order through before we set off. Oh, torches, batteries.'

'More matches.'

'Beer!' he shouted triumphantly.

'Chocolate!'

He laughed across at her, pushing the flop of his hair

away from his eyes. For a second his look lingered on her. 'I'll give you a task. Find the elephant. Then you can have your reward.'

She started running along the bank of the creek, keeping pace with *Sprite*, as happy and excited as he was now. 'George, I've just thought. What if they've already asked someone else to bring them over?'

'No-one else would come here, except Guthrie.'

'Why not?'

He waited till he was at the mouth of the creek. He manoeuvred his way into the wind, squatting under the jib as it swung across and he dodged to the other side. Then he leaned out and lifted a hand to her in farewell.

'They reckon it's haunted.'

CHAPTER TEN

Ellie dawdled her way back to the lighthouse keeper's cottage. She was smiling to herself, warm with the thoughts of their day together. *Haunted!* Trust a boy like George to try to scare her. Nothing could spoil her day now. She already loved Wild Island. The breeze was lovely, just licking the grasses and wild flowers. The day was far less oppressive than yesterday had been. Small white clouds drifted across the sky, as if they were sailing boats on the ocean. As she climbed the Height towards the house she could see the sea again on all sides, shimmering in the late-afternoon sun, every wave capped with a white mane. She flung out her arms and whirled herself round. George was right. She had fallen under the spell of the island.

She fetched her sketchbook and pencils and watercolours from her rucksack in the cottage and perched herself on the rock that she had come to think of as George's, where he always liked to eat his meal, book in one hand, fork in the other. For a time she just sat with her eyes closed, listening to the surge of the sea and the occasional melancholy cry of a sea bird. She felt completely at peace. She opened up her sketchbook and frowned at her painting of the mussel shell. 'Do better next time, Ellie.' She paused for a moment, remembering that sensation she had felt, that sense of someone watching her. She had imagined it, she smiled. George had been collecting driftwood. Forget it. She flicked the page over, smoothing her hand across the paper.

For a time she sat like that, at ease with herself. Then she began to write.

Dad. I think I am beginning to be happy again now. The last few months I have been in turmoil – you leaving, Mum bringing that awful Angus Sweatyhead home (how could she?), the exams, you going to Cornwall of all places, her marrying Angus. It's all been awful. I didn't think I would ever be happy again. But today, I am feeling different about everything. It's because I am here on this magical island, and its spell is enchanting me. While I'm here I'm going to do lots of drawings and paintings of what I find; it'll be a kind of diary. That's what you'd want me to do, isn't it? That's why I came here, because I thought you would want me to. And when I've finished here, I'm going to send it all to you as a present. So this is for you, Dad. I'm going to start with the lighthouse keeper's cottage. Notes first, just like you've taught me. Low building, faded white paint on walls. Most of it is flaking off. Stone tiled roof a bit mossy, a bit askew. Corrugated iron lean-to – that's the kitchen. Painted blue. Windows glinting in sunlight. I've noticed something particular about the kitchen. It has a window set into the door, which opens inwards because of the weather. And when it's open, the window is like a framed picture, reflecting the scene outside; the hill, the wall, the path to the bay. If you were standing by the sink with the door open, you would see anyone coming up from the shore before they reached the door. It's like having the outside inside the house. So I'll paint that for you too, some time. There are a couple of derelict outhouses. Might have been for animals at some time. George said the crofters would have kept milk cows here, chickens, maybe pigs? There's a little grass yard in front of the house. Cottage surrounded by a low tumbly-stone wall. Oh, time. Five-ish? Strong afternoon sunshine.

She stopped writing for a moment, smiled to herself. I'd like to tell someone about George too. Not Dad, perhaps. Hannah or Kasia and the twins. I wish I could just phone them up and tell them how much he's changed. He's – friendly. Now. Since we arrived here he really has been trying to look after me, in his strange way. Perhaps he's shy. I didn't like him when I first met him, or when I was travelling here on the train with him. He was always listening to his music. I thought he was rude and selfish. But since his batteries have run down (ha!) I like him better. First thing Hannah would ask would be – is he good-looking? Yes. He is. His eyes are exactly the same colour as his hair, a kind of dark nut-brown going to auburn, and it goes golden when the sun's on him.

She started writing again. *That's George's T-shirt – he towelled himself down with it after his swim this morning. I'll draw it, just as it is, draped over the wall to dry. He's left his ghost behind!*

So, Dad – meet George. I know him better than any of Morag's family – but I don't really know him at all.

She began to draw the cottage, and was soon so lost in concentration that she scarcely looked anywhere else. The sun moved westward, the light mellowed, the darkening sky turned to blood, and still she drew, until she was conscious of a crick in her neck and her back, stiff with sitting still for so long. It was growing cold. She closed her sketchbook.

At that moment, just flickering in the corner of her eye, she caught a glimpse of a long shadow retreating from the grass at her side, as if once again someone had been looking over her shoulder at her drawing.

'George! You're back!' She slid down from the boulder and hopped round. There was no-one there.

'George?' she called. 'Where are you?'

Nothing. No-one. For a brief moment fear turned her cold. She tried to shrug it away. It was a trick of light, after all. A cloud shadow. She pulled her mobile out of her pocket and clicked it on to see the time. It was nearly half past eight. *No! Surely he should be back by now?*

She ran into the cottage. Maybe she had been right, maybe he was here after all. He had looked over her shoulder and dodged silently away, to tease her. Just like yesterday.

'George?'

But there was no sign of him, no bags of shopping, no answer to her call. She left her sketch book and art stuff on the table and ran across the Height and down to the creek, hoping to see *Sprite* moored there. Her breath caught in her throat. Ebb tide, ebb tide, she chanted to herself. The sea is flowing out. High tide was over four hours ago. He must have left Kyle by now. Why isn't he here? In desperation she ran the other way, to Landlook Point. She stood cupping her hands round her eyes just as George had done earlier. Surely Kyle had a strip of sand in front of it. That meant the tide had gone out. She could see the sandbank, the treacherous sandbank, reared clean above its dangerous currents. She swept round, peering frantically for a sign of a little green boat with red sails. There were no sailing ships on the water. Not one. The sea was empty.

Now she had no idea where to look, or what to do. Keeping as close to the shore as she dared, she walked back to the creek, to the headland behind the lighthouse, to the shell beach. No sign of him or *Sprite*, or *Miss Tweedie*, or anything. There were a few container ships far, far out on the horizon. Nothing else. At last she went back to the cottage. The sky was fierce with flame, the sea seeped with scarlet.

I'm alone, she thought. *Alone on this island.* Tears streamed down her cheeks, and she could do nothing to stop them. *What has George done? It's a joke, he's played a cruel joke on me, he's as selfish and mean as I always thought he was. How could I have been taken in by him? He doesn't want me on his island. He's done it on purpose, to frighten me.*

She stood in the doorway, running her fingers through her hair, staring out at the empty sea. *Stop it, stop it*, she told herself. If you let yourself be frightened now, it's going to be much worse when it gets dark. Be logical. That's what Mum would say. Think. There could be any number of reasons why he hasn't come back. He might have misjudged the tide. He might have waited on for Bill and Morag, and, by the time they came, it was too late to cross. He might have capsized, and had to go back to Kyle. He might have capsized and *drowned*. No. Not that. Don't think that. Don't. Don't.

She allowed herself to imagine him frantically running up and down the shore at Kyle, desperately trying to drag his dinghy over wet sands into water that was too shallow to sail her. She imagined him standing knee deep in mud, his hands cupped over his eyes, searching the horizon for Wild Island.

It doesn't make any difference, does it? It doesn't matter whether he did it on purpose or not. You're still here on your own.

He'll come on the early morning tide. Twelve and a half hours between tides. About four thirty? He'll come. It won't be dark, the sun rises early. He can come then. He will. Full of apologies and worry and extra bars of chocolate. He'll come. I'll be fine.

What will you do? What on earth will you do?

I'll read till it's dark, and sleep, and get up with the sun and meet him. We'll have early breakfast watching the sun rising fully. He won't let me down. George, George, don't let me down. He won't.

She went into the kitchen to prepare herself some food, scanning the supplies in the pantry. She could open a tin of corned beef and have it with – baked beans! No problem. And then she could have – pineapple chunks. *Oh, Mum, we never have gourmet food like this at home!* She found herself humming as she prepared the meal, and thought, surprised, *I like it. I like being on my own. You're good company, Eleanor Brockhole.* The kitchen door was open. Suddenly she thought she caught a flicker of movement reflected in its window, turned her head sharply, drew in her breath, made herself go outside and stand so she could see everything; the shell beach, the path, the hillside. Of course there was nothing, no-one, of course he wouldn't be there. It was too late. *Stop watching*, she told herself. *Stop waiting*.

It was too gloomy by now to eat in the house, now the sun had dropped. She took her food outside and sat on George's boulder to eat it, facing the last red streaks of the sunset. Take your mind off it. Enjoy the light.

'Dad, you should see this,' she said aloud. 'It's as if the sun is bleeding into the water. Scarlet, would I use? Touches of yellow ochre, indigo? And pale washed green for the whole of the rest of the sky.'

'And how about the water?' she imagined him saying, and she thought of the swift, sure strokes he would make with his brush, and how he would wet it from the top down to make the colours run into each other. 'Now you do it, Ellie.'

Soon after he had moved away from home he had taken her to a loch, and they had spent the whole day just painting patches of water, catching reflections, catching sunlight, ripples, shadows, stillness. It had been a wonderful day. And then he had destroyed it. She could remember the exact moment. He was leaning over her shoulder, demonstrating with a dab of the brush how a flick of movement in the water would show against a rock. She could feel again the warmth of the hand that touched her shoulder, feel his breath on her cheek.

'Your mother and I are getting divorced, Ellie,' he had said.

She could remember how cold she felt inside, how her very skin was trembling, her heart thumping like birds' wings. 'Why?'

'It doesn't matter why. I'm leaving Scotland in the summer.'

'This summer?'

'I'm going to Cornwall.'

'Dad!' She had pushed his hand away. She could see again now the smear of white across the painting, the ruination of it. 'Don't go! You can't! Don't leave me!'

He had tried to hold her tight in his arms, but she had pummelled his chest, desperate to free herself from him and run, and at last she had given way to deep, hurt, loud sobs.

'I have to go, honey,' he whispered. 'Your mother and I can't live in the same house any more.'

'But you don't, anyway. It's all right, you living near the park. It's okay.'

'It's not okay.'

She had a question to ask him, but the words were darting fishes in dark water; couldn't be netted, couldn't be brought to light. Instead she said: 'But why Cornwall? Why so far?'

'There's not enough space for me here.'

Now Ellie put down her plate; her food unfinished. She had no taste for it any more. 'You should have come here, Dad,' she said out loud. 'Plenty of space.'

She stood up abruptly, letting her fork clatter to the ground, kicking over her mug of black tea. What was that other word, she thought? About the tide? Flood tide, high tide, ebb tide. Low tide! That's nearly now, surely. Halfway between tides. About ten o'clock. Then it'll start to flow in again. Too late to empty the loo bucket! She scraped her unfinished food into the black bin bag and knotted it firmly. I'll wash up now, she thought. That's what Mum would say. Don't mope. Be practical. Keep busy. And then, go to Landlook Point. He'll be staying at his Aunt Izzie's tonight. He's bound to signal to me with her torch. Bound to. He'll signal to tell me he's all right, so I'll know he's thinking about me. If only I had a way of signalling back. But he'll know I'm watching, looking out for him.

She half-ran in her eagerness, in her joy at the thought of the signal that she knew would be coming for her. You don't really care for him, though, she told herself. Not at all. I don't. He's very rude. He's very kind, though, when he wants to be. When he was telling me about the birds on the cliff. He's like a brother, probably. Or a cousin. Not a friend. Not that way.

Lights were beginning to come on in Kyle, so far away that they were like stars reflecting in long streaks on the damp sand on the shore. She could make out the short row of amber street lamps, the steady gleam of eyes that must be house lights. She could see the occasional moving light of a vehicle; but no flashing torch. She sat motionless while the sky deepened and some house lights were extinguished. Occasionally came the low rippling song of a late curlew heading for shore. 'Surely it's ten by now?' she wondered aloud. She let herself take a look at her mobile. Ten fifteen. No light from Aunt Izzie's. George, George, where are you? Think of me, please think of me. I'm thinking of you. Where is he? *Drowned?*

She sat another fifteen minutes, growing cold, with stars flowering into the sky, and felt rather than heard a kind of steady breathing in the air around her, as if someone was standing next to her, watching with her, waiting. *I'm frightening myself*, she thought. *Out here in the nearly dark. Go back. Go to bed. I must go back before it gets really dark. What if I can't find the cottage? Get to bed, Ellie.* But still she lingered, five minutes, ten minutes more, willing George to send her a message of light to say that he was safe, that he was thinking of her. She kept staring out at the horizon till her eyes smarted and all the last lights of Kyle seemed to be winking and dancing; till she dared stay no longer. She stood up, and looked down towards the rocks of Lone Lassie's steps.

For a brief second, it almost seemed as if there could

have been somebody standing there; a grey shape in the uneasy light, no more than that. *George?* But Ellie knew she was mistaken. Why would he stand there, and not speak or come to her?

A dark bird rose up from the sea and flew towards her, long neck looped like a snake, and perched on the rock next to her. It speared the air with its deep ungainly beak and spread out huge drooping black wings.

'Go away. Go away,' she shouted in fright, and the cormorant rose up with a guttural, raggedy cry. She stumbled back to the cottage across grass that was white with starlight, felt her way to her room, and slid thankfully into the comfort of her sleeping bag.

CHAPTER ELEVEN

For most of the night Ellie lay with her eyes wide open, staring into the darkness, listening to every sound, too afraid to let herself sleep. Yet eventually she must have drifted off, because, as on the night before, she felt a cold kiss on her cheek, and woke up, startled.

'Who's there?' she whispered.

Nothing, of course, no one. Had she been dreaming?

'Dad?'

Could she have been dreaming that Dad kissed her? Or even George? But it had felt as cold as ice. She touched her cheek. It still felt cold. Was George there, in the room with her, standing silent and still? She reached out, groping into the nothingness of the grey of early dawn, staring at shapes that melted and swam into that utter nothingness. She sank back, closing her eyes, remembering that she was alone in a tiny cottage on a small island, surrounded by the sea, the weeping, surging, rolling, endless sea, the fishes and birds, the dragging weeds, the shifting sands, the creeping shells of the sea. And as she tried to drift back towards her lonely slumber she imagined she heard the sound of somebody sighing, and the light step of somebody moving away from her over the bare floorboards.

She lay tight still, her heart pounding wildly. There's nothing there, she told herself. There's nobody here. She strained with all her nerves to hear the sound again. It was my own breathing. It was the movement of my sleeping bag on the floor. A mouse in the corner. A bird on the roof. It was the beating of my own heart.

She stayed wide awake now, listening, watching; hearing and seeing nothing, until the dawn light began to suffuse the room, and then pulled herself out of her sleeping bag. She hadn't undressed the night before, except for her sandals. Now she pulled them on and padded through to the kitchen. Of course it was empty, and there was no sign that anyone had been there. She went out of the cottage. A pink dawn was streaking the sky, and she remembered the early tide. George would be on it. He would have set his alarm at his Aunt Izzie's. 'You can't leave the girl there on her own,' his aunt would have told him. 'Take the supplies now and go out to her on the early tide.'

'He'll bring eggs,' Ellie said aloud. 'And bacon, beautiful juicy salty bacon, and orange juice with bits in it, and lovely soft bread with a brown crust. And butter just the right temperature for spreading. And honey from the bees that feed on the heather.' She chanted a list of breakfasts out loud, remembering eggs collected still warm from the hens at her grandfather's allotment, remembering the smell of freshly baked bread from the machine at home. She would go to Landlook Point and keep watch, and as soon as she spied *Sprite* she would run over the Height to the creek to meet the little boat. She dared to hope that George would be on his own. She would help him to carry the supplies home, and they would cook breakfast together and eat it sitting on the boulders outside the cottage. She wouldn't be angry with him. She wouldn't ask why he hadn't come yesterday, or why he hadn't flashed a torch from Aunt Izzie's to say *Good night, all's well*. She wouldn't mention that she'd been frightened. She wouldn't even tell him that she'd watched out for him.

There were a few boats already leaving on the early tide. Through her spy-glassed hands she watched them as they drew near enough for her to make out their colours. Fishing boats, she knew that. No pea-green dinghy with taut red sails. Nothing that looped round after the sandbanks to veer towards the island. How long must she wait and watch? How long must she listen to the mocking call of the herring gulls and know that the tide had turned and was on the ebb, and still no boat coming, no *Sprite* leaning into the wind and casting its cloud of spindrift?

By mid-morning the sun was heavy and full. Ellie didn't know the exact time because her phone was very low on battery and she had turned it off, not wanting to use it up unless she really had to. She had spent the morning dozing, lying on the grass in front of the cottage. She had hardly slept at all the night before, and was still sludgy with lack of sleep. She decided to go down to the creek and paint a picture of it for her father. Yesterday George's little boat *Sprite* was moored there. *Yesterday!* Already it seemed like weeks ago. Yesterday the creek was full of sunlight. Yesterday she had swum in the lagoon in water that was so clear and blue that she could see rippled sand beneath her, shoals of tiny darting silver fish. She saw *Sprite*. In the creek that fed the lagoon she definitely saw *Sprite*. She knew she had done. She knew this was the same place. And yet, everything had shifted to a different scene, a different light. And just where *Sprite* was moored – she *knew* it was there! – there was instead an old rotting boat – a rowing boat, small and black with dried-up strands of seaweed draping over the sides like shredded curtains.

She sank down onto the grass, staring, her heart thumping, her throat dry and clenched with fear. And yet she couldn't pull herself away. She was too frightened to move. Slowly, afraid to make a sound, she opened up her sketchbook and folded back a new page. She felt in the bag for a pencil, never taking her eyes off the black boat. And then she began to write.

Dad. I have to tell you this. I have to paint you something that was not there yesterday. I have to paint you something that is not beautiful, but ugly. Frightening. Believe me, Dad.

Notes: water brackish, quite still, as if the tide that feeds it hasn't reached it for weeks. Dark brown like the Guinness that you love. Scud. Scummy. Flies and midges. Slimy weeds. Nearly black, creamy round the rocks. A black boat. A cormorant on its bows, stretching out its black umbrella wings. There – something bulged up in the water, but it's too dark to see what it is. A seagull screams, but I can't paint a scream, can I?

Faster she wrote, faster, the words hardly decipherable now. *There is a painting of a scream; I remember now. There's that famous painting, the one that was stolen. The man standing on a bridge screaming, with his hands cupped round his face, and all the wavy lines and streaky sky. Everything unreal, like fairground mirrors distorting.*

Ellie put down her pencil, remembering the time that her father had taken her to a fairground, and how she had cried to go in a dodgem car. She had sat on his knee, steering round and round in an ecstasy of madness, until a boy in a blue car had rammed hers, and she had broken her tooth on the steering wheel. Dad had carried her home, shoulder high. She remembered screaming, high-pitched screaming, looking down to see blood on her new pink dress. Mum had said it didn't matter. She would be growing another tooth soon anyway. Fairground. Fairground screams.

Munch, that was the painter. And her father said *The Scream* was a bit of a cliché now because everyone knows it and children wear masks of it at Halloween. He showed her a painting of a different scream, a man in a glass box, his whole mouth open like a square, all his teeth showing, and rage in his face. The artist was Francis Bacon. That's me, she thought. I'm imprisoned in a box made of glass, and no-one can hear me screaming. Except that the man in the glass box wasn't terrified. He was creating terror.

She began to paint, fiercely flourishing her brush so that not one line was solid or real, hardly glancing any more at the scene that she was trying to represent but looking only at the page she was working on with its swaying, vibrant, intense colours. And when she did look across at the rotting boat again, she saw its veil of black seaweed lifting slightly, falling again. She saw the name painted on its side. *Spectre.*

Ellie snapped shut her paint-box and stood up. I have to be practical about this. I've come to the wrong creek, that's all. Why would George bother to show me this creek, with an old rotten boat in it, when he wanted to show me *Sprite*, and he wanted to swim? He told me this island is full of hidden coves. I've just come to the wrong place, that's all. She started to climb back up the slope, holding her painting in front of her to let it dry. The light was changing; she was walking into sunlight, the air was lighter, lovelier. Don't look back. I must be practical. I must make the day normal again. Eat. That's it. I must eat. This is my home till someone comes for me. And they will. George will come on the evening tide. Five o'clock-ish this evening. Of course he will. It's only two tides he's missed. Yesterday afternoon he didn't have enough time – too much to do, too little time. And the other one was in the middle of the night, for goodness' sake. He simply didn't wake up in time. But this time, this time, he will come. He will. George. Please, George. Please, please.

She cooked up the remainder of the corned beef with some spaghetti – 'Nothing but the best!' – and took it outside to his boulder. The food was gone too quickly. She washed up and then tried to pump more water. It was so tiring that she only brought up enough to wash her hands and face before she exhausted herself. She sank down, dispirited, and after a while of moodily staring at the red bucket she stood, gritted her teeth, and tried again. Once she got into a rhythm it was easier, and she began to sing. She tried to think of a shanty but couldn't, so she made one up:

'Water come and water go

Yo ho heave ho yo ho ho

Slosh it down and splash my toe

Yo ho heave ho yo ho ho!'

Her voice chimed out, thin and brave and breathless, until the bucket was half-full and she knew it was just about the right weight for her to carry.

'And I won't need more. George will bring bottles and bottles of it. And if he doesn't he can pump the next lot!'

When she arrived back at the cottage she knew she had to find something to do to fill the time. She went into a flurry of rummaging to see what she could find. 'I'm having a nosy, George. Do you mind?' She opened all the drawers, and cupboards, and finally the chest, where everything had been stored away against the mice. She found books of poetry, novels, bird books, jigsaw puzzles, Scrabble, a box of chess, and the binoculars that George had promised her were there. She slung them round her neck, then picked out a lined exercise book. It was full of poems or maybe songs, half-finished, full of crossings-out and scribblings. Bill Donaldson's? Or George's? She closed the book hurriedly. Maybe she shouldn't be prying into something so personal. Instead, she opened one of the sea bird books. She flicked through the pages, reading out loud a litany of their names.

'Kittiwake. Fulmar. Cormorant. Herring gull. Gannet. Guillemot. Razor Bill and puffin. Great black-blacked gull. Whoops! Did it again! Can never say that one!' *I'll study them*, she thought. *I'll use the binoculars to identify them, and I'll learn their names and their ways, and I'll paint them for Dad.*

The tide still hadn't turned, the sun was still high overhead. She guessed it must be about noon. How slowly the day was creeping. She picked up her sketch pad and pencils, and wandered idly and sleepily along the old tracks, exploring the island, making her way down to the little coves that had become exposed by the low tide. The granite rocks had weird formations. As she approached one, an elephant's trunk seemed to emerge out of the rock. An elephant! She ran towards it and eventually saw what George had asked her to look for – a rock twenty-foot high or more, exactly formed like an elephant, its trunk dipped in a pool, tufts of grass above its eyes and along its back.

'Hello, Hairy Mammoth. I won't draw something else for Dad, I'll draw you for George. I won't say anything, just prop the drawing up in the kitchen and demand my reward!'

She sat down and opened out her sketchbook, but her pencil stayed still on the page. She was too restless, too anxious to spend any time on drawing. She had no heart for it any more.

At last she allowed herself to go back to Landlook Point. She knew it was still not time for high tide, and that there was no chance at all that George would have been able to launch *Sprite* yet. Even so, she would watch the tide flooding in, she would see the little fleet of boats that would be launching soon from Kyle, and through her binoculars she would be able to follow the sail as red as rust that would be *Sprite*. She imagined George sitting on the wall of the prom, his long legs swinging, plugged in again to his music because he would have charged up his iPod at Aunt Izzie's, running his fingers through his floppy hair; thinking, wondering, waiting. Maybe, if he was with Bill and Morag, he would have brought the stronger binoculars from the car and would be training them on the island, scanning it for her. They would meet, binocular to binocular, and wave, and smile.

She allowed herself to imagine this, even though she knew that the distance between Kyle and Wild Island would be far too great even for Bill's binoculars, and that the little ones she was carrying round her neck had just simple magnification for close bird-watching. She knew all that, and yet she stood on Landlook Point and lifted them to her eyes and focused them on the dark blur that was mainland. She couldn't even make out buildings. Disappointed, she swung the binoculars to the sandbank, still cleared of water like a whale's back, and could see the gleam of the moat with its treacherous, impossible currents. In the afternoon light the water was lapping the sand as though it had no malice in its heart at all. More than ever, it looked possible to wade across to the bank. Would a strong swimmer make it across the moat? What if she did it? She could wave to the people on the mainland. She could signal with something. Even, perhaps, wade across from there. So there were sinking sands, George had said. But she could test them, she could take a stick with her and test them before every step she made. It might be possible, if she got desperate. *Never, never even try.*

Ellie moved the binoculars along the sandbanks. Now she could make out a dark shape there. Surely she would have seen it before? What was it? She turned the focus wheel on the binoculars, frustrated because the magnification was so weak. A person? A dog? A post? She had no sense of scale, nothing to measure it against to give her a sense of its height. It wasn't moving. Or was it? She lowered her binoculars, and then something else caught her eye.

Below her, on Lone Lassie's stones, a girl was standing, staring as Ellie had been towards the sandbanks. Ellie gasped aloud. She stepped forward, and instantly the shape that had been a girl became a shadow, a darkening of the water, a wisp of nothing.

It's with peering so long through the binoculars, Ellie told herself. *My eyes have gone blurry. There's nothing there. No-one.*

Uneasy, she turned away from it, turned her back on the Lone Lassie's stones and the sandbank and mainland.

She was extraordinarily tired. Lack of sleep can give you delusions, she told herself. All I want to do is sleep. Sleep. She curled up in the grass, just for a moment, feeling the benediction of sunlight on her, its soothing warmth. She could hear the sweet cry of the oystercatchers wading on the muddy strand. She could hear the long, sighing breath of the sea. 'This is a magic place, remember,' she whispered. Sleep, sleep, and when you wake up, all will be well.

Ellie had no idea what time it was when she woke up, stiff and cold, at Landlook Point. The sun and its warmth had gone, most of the light had gone, and a cold, damp mist swirled round her. As soon as she began to climb away from the point the mist thickened; she could hardly distinguish boulders in front of her. Alarmed, she tried to make her way by memory towards the cottage, keeping well away from the cliffs. The birds were silent. The hiss of the sea was muted.

'He can't come now,' she muttered. 'Not in a fog. Surely he wouldn't set sail in a fog. And, anyway, surely the tide has been and gone.'

She only realised that she had completely lost her way when she could just distinguish a massive white bulk looming out of the grey, a grim and ghostly finger of warning; the lighthouse.

Out of the low building behind it suddenly came a deafening high-pitched moan; it seemed to come from its very throat. Ellie put her hands over her ears as she drew near to the building. There it came again, an unearthly wail. And again it came, blasting from hell, like the shriek of a woman's cry of grief. She stumbled past the terrifying sound, head down, and then paused, shaking. If she was near the lighthouse, she must be near the edge of the cliff where the cormorants lived; where a keeper had lost his way in the fog and dropped to his death onto the rocks below. Now she felt blind with fear, faint with it, dumb with it, too frightened to cry out. She dropped down on her hands and knees, clutching the grass and the earth and rocks beneath her fingers, feeling her way forward inch by inch, blindly into the mist, until she realised that she was climbing and had reached the summit of the Height. She trusted herself then to stand up and walk instead of crawling, sure that she must be heading the right way now. She blundered forward, hands groping for nothing, and suddenly made out a flickering orange light coming towards her, like a torch.

'Hello! Hello! I'm here!' Ellie called, and her voice was

a strangled, muffled sound in the mist. It wasn't a torch. She could just make out the dim shape of a building. The light was coming from the windows of the cottage, surely. It was! She began to run, steadily now, tearful with relief, and flung open the door. The fire had been lit. Bright, welcoming flames danced in the brick hearth.

CHAPTER TWELVE

George had nosed *Sprite* into the shore of Kyle bay after
leaving Ellie on Wild Island. He jumped out and hauled his
boat up onto the crinkly white shingle. Two little barefoot
boys ran to help him, dancing and *ow!*-ing as the sharp
cockleshells tickled their feet. It had been a perfect afternoon
for a sail. He looked back at the distant island, pleased with
himself, pleased with the fact that he had decided to sail
over that day.

'I wish Ellie had come, though. I must get her to try
it tomorrow,' he said to himself. 'Perhaps she really was
nervous about sailing with me.' She seemed so shy. She
hadn't wanted to swim that morning, he remembered, but
while she thought he wasn't looking she had slipped into
the lagoon and turned over and over in the water, easy as
a fish, before she floated on her back. I wish I hadn't just
gone off like that. Too shy to stay, too anxious about how she

would look when she stepped out of the water, like a little mermaid with streaming hair. I was embarrassed. *Me*! She's quite sweet, really.

His usual beaching place for *Sprite* had been taken by some kayaks, so he had pulled in much further along the beach. He and the boys pulled the boat up behind the lifeboat house, well away from sight. The last thing George wanted was for someone to take a fancy to her and sail off before he returned from Molly Duncan's shop. He reckoned he had a maximum of two hours on shore before he had to set back again. Loads of time really. He strolled along the beach and then jumped up onto the prom, dusted the glistening sand away from his feet and put his sandals back on. He bought himself an ice cream and sat dangling his legs over the wall while he ate it. A herring gull tried to dive bomb him, pink legs stuck out in front, huge grey wings flapping. 'Gerroff,' he shouted. 'It's mine!'

He remembered then that the first thing he should have done was to contact his dad, and he wandered along the prom with his ice cream in one hand and his mobile in the other, searching for a signal. Just outside Molly's shop he got reception. There were eight missed calls and three messages, all from his father.

'Is that George?'

He turned round to see Molly waving to him from the shop doorway. 'You're here at last! I have a box of provisions for you, that your mother phoned through the other day. It's all ready!'

'Great!' he said. 'I'll collect it before I go back. Could you add a few bottles of beer? Oh, and a couple of bars of chocolate?'

'Aye, I'll do that. But don't forget to collect it, mind!'

He waved his thanks to her and turned away to open the most recent message from his father.

Where the hell are you? Phone me at once. Urgent.

He dropped his melting ice cream into the litter bin outside Molly's shop. The gull screamed at him. George's hands were shaking as he pressed return call. There was no reply. Maybe his father was just being melodramatic because he hadn't gone to Izzie's as he had instructed. But maybe it was more than that. Maybe there was a crisis at home. Mum on her bike. Oh God.

'Dad? What's up?' He spoke to the answer phone, then he texted the same message. He tried phoning home. There was no reply. He tried his mother's mobile. Again, no reply, and again he left a message. By now he was in a state of helpless panic. He rang Aunt Izzie's number, waited till the answer phone message came on, then blurted out, 'Aunt Iz, it's George. I'm here, in Kyle. I'm staying on the island. I'm okay. Can you let Dad know?'

He sat on the wall of the prom, his head in his hands, not knowing what to do next. Again and again he repeated the sequence of calls, and at last his phone rang and he heard his father's voice.

'George? George?'

'I'm here, Dad.'

'George? Can you hear me?'

Gulls screamed round him, chased by shrieking children. George crossed to the other side of the road.

'George?'

'Dad, I can hear you now. What's up? What's happening? Why haven't you come?'

'George, stop! Stop babbling. Listen. It's serious. Stop talking.'

'Okay.' There was a bench against the wall. He lowered himself down onto the seat. His hands were sticky with sweat. 'I'm listening.'

'Mo is seriously ill.'

'She wasn't well in the car.'

'LISTEN! We don't know what it is, but she's unconscious in the hospital. I had to take her straight there when I left you. Her condition is critical, George. You've got to come home.'

George closed his eyes. His whole body was shaking now, weak with shock. His father's voice wound into his ear, the words breaking up. '. . . She may not pull through. Come at once . . . Straight to the Royal . . . Intensive Care. Mum's here with Izzie. You've got money?'

'Yes. You gave me loads.' Alert now, George fished in his pocket. 'Plenty.'

'Get home at once. We need you – your mum needs you. And Morag does.' His father was crying. George felt sobs rising in his throat. 'Going back in now. Get here as quick as you can.'

'I'll come. I'll come.'

The contact was lost.

Chapter Thirteen

Dad. I'm going to paint something I've never painted before, but first I want to record two things because I can't make sense of them. The first was so sudden and frightening that I thought my heart was going to leap out of my body. The other was so kind and lovely and welcoming that it made me want to cry. But I can't find an explanation for either of them. This is my third night on the island, the second completely on my own. At first I hated everything. I wash myself with water that I've had to pump up from a well; I don't change my clothes even though I swam in them yesterday. I cook food out of tins. I sleep in a room that's drumming with the tiny sound of mice. But it's not that – all that is nothing to me now. Dad, I hear sounds and see shadows. I saw an old boat that wasn't there before. I saw someone standing on the rocks, and then I couldn't see her at all. I can hear sighing, whispering, moving, as if the air around me is shifting.

Now strange things are happening all the time; more and more of them; more and more frightening. I feel as if I'm living a nightmare. Inexplicable things startle me; scare me out of my wits. I can't pretend they're not happening any more. When George told me the island was haunted, I thought he was teasing me. Now I think he was right. I don't know how I'm managing to open my eyes or stand on my feet or move from one side of the room to the other, let alone across the island, yet I do. I keep going.

And at the same time I can read and draw and paint and wander in the most beautiful place I have ever seen. This island is enchanted, George told me. It's a magical place. You'd love it. And, in spite of everything that's happened, I do.

But tonight, when the fog was wreathing round me like cold, damp sweat, and it had come out of nowhere, and I nearly lost my way home - home! - to the cottage, I could hardly breathe for fear. And then there came a shriek like a mad woman's voice that seemed to rise up out of the earth, again and again and again.

But I found the cottage and there was the most wonderful thing. Someone had lit a fire in the grate! The room is filled with its soft golden glow, and its warmth, and its whispering.

Shadows are flickering round the walls of the room like friendly creatures.

'Who lit it?' she asked herself again. 'George? But there's no sign of him. Has he lit it and gone looking for me? And where are the supplies he went for? Nothing makes sense. Nothing.'

I've never painted fire before. You've never shown me how to do it. So I'm looking into its colours. Red, orange, yellow, blue, green. I'm looking at the shapes of the fire creatures, how they dance and bend and curl and leap; how they have soft faces with huge, black mouths and winking eyes. I'm going to paint them for you now. I'm painting firelight by firelight. You'll see how friendly it makes the room now, and how beautiful, and you'll know that I'm not afraid any more.

When I've finished painting it, I'm not going to go down the narrow, cold passage to the room I sleep in. I'm going to curl up in front of the fire. I can hear that voice shrieking outside, regular and moaning, and I know what it is now. This is the lighthouse-keeper's cottage; of course. What I can hear is the foghorn, warning ships about the rocks.

In the very early hours of the morning, the foghorn stopped. It was the stopping that woke Ellie up from her restless sleep. She lay in the stillness of the half-light listening to the heaving breath of the sea and the early clamour of gulls. *Today*, she thought, *I will be rescued*.

The fire had long gone out. George's sleeping bag was scrunched on the settee from the first night. She unrolled it and climbed into it, enjoying the luxury of its warmth around her, drifting in and out of a comfortable sleep. She dreamt of the sea, and when she woke up she lay listening to it, breathing with it, in tune and in rhythm with it, as if she had become part of it, as if the sea coursed through her veins.

Today, George will tire of the silly game he's playing. Wherever he is, he'll phone someone to come and rescue her. Perhaps he told Morag what he had done. She would be furious with him; she'd get the lifeboat out, or Guthrie, anyone, to bring Ellie off the island. Both the families would know by now. There might be a report of it in the local papers: '*Student prank leaves schoolgirl marooned on deserted island*.' It might make the national news. Someone might make a film of it one day. She changed the newspaper headline to 'Marooned on Haunted Island'. It would be on everybody's Facebook page, and when she stepped off the lifeboat onto land at Kyle there would be crowds waving banners; there would be reporters and cameramen. And would she be magnanimous in her forgiveness of George Donaldson? No, she would not.

Maybe her mother will have been brought back from her honeymoon. She would be interviewed on the TV news. Ellie tried to imagine her, tense and white-faced; the camera would show her wreathing her hands together, twisting her new white-gold wedding ring. Her hair would be loose and slightly unkempt, as an indication of the trauma that she herself had been through. She would have forgotten to touch up her roots with mascara, and she would be without make-up. Actually, that was the way Angus Sweatyhead seemed to prefer her; she was growing out her hair dye to please him. Now that was quite remarkable, come to think of it. He was certainly having a major influence on her. *Hey, Mum*, Ellie thought. *Who are you now? Do I really know you any more?* She would think about that later. Meanwhile, she drifted back to the story, the television news interview. 'She was always a nervous child,' her mother would say. 'Deeply sensitive. This experience will have traumatised her.'

'Don't be silly, Mum.' Ellie clambered out of the sleeping bag. Day had come fully now; the sun poured honey light into the room. 'You know nothing about it. You abandoned

me so you could go and have fun with your shiny boyfriend.'
She thought of Angus in his running gear, steaming into the
house, clicking his watch to check how long his jog through
the parks had taken this time, shouting out his triumph.
She thought of her mother twining her silky hands into
his sweaty ones, smiling at him, ordering him to sweeten
himself up in the shower.

She pulled on a sweatshirt and went into the pantry.
The food was lined up on the shelves like an army of stocky
tin soldiers, smart and brightly coloured and ready for
inspection. She knew all their names off by heart now.

'Eat healthily,' she imagined her mother saying.
'Choose some tinned fruit, but not in syrup. You need your
vitamin C.'

Ellie scrutinised the labels on the tins. 'Blackcurrants
in apple juice. That good enough for you, Mum? Won't get
scurvy now.'

'Carbs,' came her mother's voice again.

'Can't do it. Not out of tins. Oh – semolina? That might
do. Calcium in it too, so my teeth won't drop out.' She
opened the tins and spooned some of the contents into a
bowl. On a real desert island, she thought, there wouldn't be
a tin opener. She would have to gash the tins on a rock and

pour the contents down her throat; blackcurrants spilling their delicious purple juices all over her sweatshirt, semolina globbing like frog spawn down her chin. She took her bowl outside and ate hungrily, overhearing her mother boasting on the phone that Ellie had always been a good eater. 'She loved food from the day I weaned her. She never has the silly food fads that some teenage girls get. And look at her, as thin as a pencil.'

'It's because I've always made sure she has good food, not rubbish,' Ellie continued for her. 'Anyway, Mum, today is the last day of tinned foods. Today I'm going to be rescued.' She put her bowl and spoon on the ground. Her eyes were burning. *I will not, will not cry*, she thought. *I will not let myself cry*.

And, because her head was full of her mother's voice, she had a vivid picture of the day her mother had come into her bedroom and told her that she was going to marry Angus. She had never revisited that moment till now, never allowed herself to. Yet today while the gulls were swooping down to finish off her breakfast, she heard again the slight tap on the door, watched her mother come into her room, pulled herself up in her bed to receive a mug of coffee that her mother had brought in with her. That should have been a warning. Why coffee, in bed, especially on a school day? Instead of leaving it on Ellie's bedside table and going to get herself ready for work, Mum had sat on the edge of the bed. That was the first day that Ellie had noticed that her mother had flecks of grey in her hair.

'Mum, have you stopped dying your hair?'

'I have. I'm letting it grow out.'

'Why? I like you with dark hair.'

'Ellie, I don't want to talk to you about my hair. I want to tell you something.'

She paused, and into the silence came the sound of a blackbird singing in the tree outside Ellie's window; such a pure, sweet, effortless sound. Nothing went wrong in a blackbird's world. Ellie watched the dance of leaves through the window, how they showed their pale undersides to the wind, how they lifted themselves and fell like waves. She felt herself sinking; she felt cold, even though her hands were clasped round the mug of coffee. She heard her breath shaking.

'I know. Dad's going to live in England. He told me.' She put her mug down on the table, using both her hands so the coffee didn't spill. 'He's got a job there. But I don't want him to go.' She turned away, pulling her quilt around her shoulders, covering herself into a cocoon, curling up inside the warm cave it made. Mum put a hand on her shoulder, trying to ease the quilt away. Ellie shrugged her off. 'It's all because of Angus. You and Angus. I don't want to lose my dad.'

'You won't lose your dad.' Another pause. Somewhere in town, a police siren sounded, like a wail of pain. 'Ellie, listen. That isn't what I was going to tell you. Angus and I are getting married.'

Ellie closed her eyes. *I don't want to know*, she thought. *I don't want to hear this.*

'We love each other. You have to try to understand that. You're sixteen now.'

'You loved Dad once.' If her mother heard her, she didn't respond. Maybe that was a room she didn't want to go into any more; maybe she had closed the door on that part of her life.

'It's going to be a very quiet wedding. Just a couple of witnesses; Angus's family; you. We'll have a simple meal together afterwards.'

'You can't marry him. You're not even divorced yet!' Ellie shouted. She wanted to hurt her mother, wanted to make her feel the grief she felt.

'We are. It's over,' she told her. 'We're getting divorced.'

That was just what Dad had said. It's over. Over for him. Over for Mum. *But not for me*, Ellie thought. *I'm still married to both of them. I'm their child. I'm their daughter.*

'Is there anything else you want to ask me?' Mum said.

Ellie was silent. Of course there was, but there were no words for it. She shook her head.

'After the wedding,' her mother went on, calmly, too calmly, 'Angus and I are going on holiday. We're going to France.' She was smoothing the quilt cover as she spoke, picking at loose strands of cotton as though she had a desperate need to tidy things up, to make everything beautiful. 'We'd like you to come with us.'

'No.'

'We'd love you to come. Both of us would.'

'No.'

'We can't leave you on your own.'

'I'm sixteen, as you just reminded me.'

'No, Ellie.' Her mother stood up. 'We're all going. I want you to get to know Angus properly. This is the best way to do it. We'll share our lovely holiday together.' She bent down, trying to touch Ellie's hand, but she pulled away. For a moment they both held their silence. There was a rift between them that was like a physical wound. And then, finally, Mum left the room, used the bathroom, and got herself ready for work. Ellie didn't move until she heard the car scrunching down the drive.

CHAPTER FOURTEEN

'Today I'm going to be rescued,' Ellie told herself again. She washed and took the dreadful slop bucket down to the water's edge, judged that the tide was going out, and flung the contents into a retreating suck of wave. There were two boats on the water. The blue one, far out, could be Guthrie's. *He's like me*, she thought. *Alone on the tide, day after day. I wonder what he thinks about all day? I wonder if he talks to himself like I do.* 'And when you come home with your day's catch, Guthrie, do you always eat fish?'

I'm getting as bad my grandmother. Talking to myself out loud. She talks to the teapot, the toaster, the television. 'I'll talk to anything that doesn't answer back!' Nan used to say cheerfully. No, Nan. You talk to anything because you can't stand the silence in your own house. You have to hear a human voice, even if it's your own. I understand that now.

As she climbed back up to the cottage, Ellie realised

that she should make a flag to attract Guthrie's attention. Why on earth hadn't she thought of that before? She saw George's white T-shirt still draped over the wall. That would be perfect.

'George, I will sacrifice you to the gods. I will put a stake through your heart.'

There were no trees on the island, no useful branches. She thought about last night's fire; burned away this morning, no ash, leaving no sign that it had ever been there. But it had been there, a fire of logs, like the ones her mother bought in for Christmas. She remembered George telling her that they lit a fire in the hearth most nights after the sun went down. What would they use to burn, she had asked him, and he had told her how they combed the little beaches for the driftwood of old boats and wave-tossed branches carried by the tides. She went from one tiny beach to another, searching, finding nothing big enough or sharp enough. Everything she found was too small for a stake, but would do for firewood. Perhaps, if she still hadn't been rescued by night-time, she could make a huge fire like a beacon on the highest point of the island. It would be seen for miles. Someone would be sure to see it, and help would come.

And the smaller bits I can take back to the cottage; just

in case no-one comes – but they will! – I can light another fire tonight. She paused, her hand trembling against her lips. Footsteps with no trace. Ice-cold kisses, glimpses of shadows, sighs drifting into air, and fire that left no ash. Who lit that fire last night? Who lit it for me? And why was there nothing left of it today – no half-burnt logs, no smouldering smoke, no pile of dead ashes? Nothing. Only her painting to remember it was there at all.

In physics once at school they had learnt about phosphorescence, how it looked like light on water sometimes, and how damp wood can sometimes dance with light like real flames. Was that what it was? A natural phenomenon, after all? And yet – it had warmed her. Or was that because she had wanted it to? Like taking a placebo. It makes you better because you want it to, even though it has no medical properties. Or a mirage, where people wandering in a desert think they can see an oasis, green and shimmering, but there's nothing there. Only hope.

Don't think about it. Move on!

Collecting driftwood, she thought, was like picking blackberries. There seems to be nothing there, and the more you look, the more you find, bright eyes winking cheerfully through the thorny brambles, crying, 'Pick me! And me!

And me!' She soon had her arms loaded with knobbly bits of bleached wood that would at least serve for a hearth fire. She imagined the little boy that George had been, intent on his driftwood collection, sorting it out into different lengths to make his smuggler's lugger. She wandered round the little coves as long as she dared, until she was aware of the hush of the tide and knew that it had begun to turn. And as she climbed up the sand, away from the edge of the water, she found a narrow-mouthed cave. She peered in. Out of the darkness loomed a heap of white shapes, and surely, at the very back, a spar of wood that would be just right for her flagpole. She heaped her pile of driftwood outside the cave mouth and ventured in. The closer in she went, the more the shapes looked like white bones and skulls, even though she knew that they would be stones and shells and bits of wood that the waves had rolled in and dumped there. Or maybe George had piled them there, years ago, playing a gruesome game of dead pirates or something.

There was a sudden scream and flurry around her head. Gulls flung themselves out of the darkness, shrieking out at her, screeching their alarm and anger, and Ellie staggered backwards away from them, feeling the cold air of their wing beats around her hair, shielding her face with one hand, her elbow bent above her head. She crouched down, sobbing with fright.

'You can't scare me,' she shouted. 'You're only birds!'

'They're like the mice in the cottage. This is their home,' she told herself. 'Only birds, Ellie.'

Then, quickly, before the gulls came back and claimed their home again, she ran inside the cave. She needed that spar of wood leaning next to the bone pile. She dragged it out into the daylight, into the warm sun. It was a long plank, maybe from a wrecked ship. It was ideal. She dragged it to a different sandy bay, where she felt sure boats passing the island from the mainland would see it. She took it down to the edge of the beach and scooped away the soft sand with her hands. The more she scooped, the more sand trickled back to fill the space. She searched round for a sharp stone to use as a tool, and dug with that into the heavy wet sand below the surface. Again and again the hole filled up with water. She moved to different spots, and finally found a crack between two boulders where she could wedge the stake. Now she untied George's T-shirt from around her waist. *I love the mud at Glastonbury*, it read. She stretched it as tightly as she could against the sharp end of the stake until she had pierced a hole in the middle of the word *love*. Then she jammed the stake between the boulders.

'There, Dad. What do you think of that? Hey, Mum, I bet you didn't think your scaredy-cat daughter could do it, did you? I bet you thought I'd just lie down and cry.'

The flag T-shirt hung limply. 'Blow, wind, blow!' she shouted. 'Fly for me, flag!'

It will, she told herself. When the tide turns, the flag will fly and my rescuer will see it and come and save me.

She was spattered with mud. She paddled into the sea, letting the soft water splash up to her knees, let it creep softly and lovingly higher and higher up her body; felt it caressing her skin. She lay back with her eyes closed and floated in it; rising, falling, rising, falling, gentle as sleep. Then she lay on the sand to let the sun dry her.

Hungry now, she thought dreamily. What shall I eat, Mum? Protein. Calcium. Tinned sardines. Peas. Sugars, vitamins, carbs. Finish the semolina and the blackcurrants. I'll eat like a princess. I'm fine. I'll be fine. And today I'm going to be rescued.

She sat up, gazing out at the huge, shimmering sea, and saw her rescuer approaching.

CHAPTER FIFTEEN

Dad. I'm sitting in my cove. This is where my flag flies. This is where my rescuer arrived. I watched him for ages, just a dark blob at first, head bobbing in the silver waves, swimming, stopping, taking breath, dipping under, disappearing for minutes on end, bobbing up again, swimming slowly and steadily towards me. I stood up and waved to him. I danced up and down on the beach. It never occurred to me for one minute to wonder why he would come to me swimming rather than in a boat. It never occurred to me to wonder how he would rescue me, carry me back to land and safety and home. It didn't occur to me, not for ages, that his head wasn't the shape of a human head, that those huge dark eyes weren't human eyes. I saw shiny black skin and thought I was seeing someone in a wetsuit. I was so sure, you see, that I was going to be rescued today. This had to be my rescuer. I even dared to think that it might be George, strong swimmer

George, swum all the way from Kyle. But at last I had to admit to myself that this was no human. What then? A dog?

As soon as I realised what it was, I ran back to the cottage, grabbed my sketching stuff and the binoculars and raced back to the cove. Even though my rescuer hadn't come, not yet, I was excited. It was a sign, surely a sign of hope. So I wanted to record it for you. I was just in time to see it slither out of the sea and onto the rocks. It was a seal. I've never seen a real one before, but I remember the stories you've told me about how they sing to each other, how they wrap their flippers round each other for love. I remember the story of the selkie girl who shed her seal-skin and became a human until she found it again, and how she danced on the blue shell sand like I did earlier.

I'm going to try to paint a picture of this seal for you, so you'll know the magic of this island.

Background; sea. Gallivanting (your word!) waves, steely blue streaked with silver. Froths of spray against the rocks. Rocks – black/brown, creamy with foam. Green weeds swaying into the lapping water, fronds and furls and frills. So many shades of green, like leaves of different trees. What are the colours of green? Jade, emerald, mint, olive, apple, can't think of any more, none of them quite right. Mix, mix, mix! Must paint in those *silver-purple mussel shells on the shore. And there on the slab of rock, my seal, dark elephant grey, black patches, gleaming sea colours. Nose/snout like a dog, huge baby eyes deep deep ocean black/brown. Whiskers. Time of day - no idea. Long past noon, because the sun is casting shadows. Good light.*

Oh, Dad! His family has come! Two more - no, three, clambering slithering flopping rolling clumsy ugly beautiful seals.

When Ellie at last put the lids on her paints and stored them back in their box, the wind was getting up and her flag was flying. The seals slipped back into the water and plunged out of sight. Now and again a head bobbed up and away again. They were leaving her.

She went back to the cottage and ate, allowing herself to fantasise about bulging, sizzling sausages, onion gravy and mashed potatoes. Warm plum crumble, she went on dreamily. And then fresh strawberries, huge plump ones straight from the garden, oozing with juices. When I get home. When I'm rescued. And I will be. Today.

Home - She wrote carefully in her sketchbook - *I miss home. I miss the trees. I miss the songbirds of our garden, the thrush tugging worms out of the soil, the finches and bluetits swinging on the feeder, the robin scavenging after their dropped crumbs. These island birds are huge and loud and wailing like lost souls.*

There are so many things I miss, she thought. People, mostly. Dad and Mum, the way things used to be. Nan, of course Nan, and the wobbly wardrobe she left me from her house. My room – oh, how I miss my room. And my friends: Hannah and Kasia specially. And smiley Tess and the twins – the two for the price of one friends, buy one get one free, bubbles of private jokes and laughter. What would they all think of it here? It would be a joke, if they were all here with me. We'd scream ourselves silly and then go into hysterics of laughter and it would be all right.

I even miss Tommy and Leo, really the only boys worth knowing in our class. Before George. I don't know anyone quite like him.

She started scribbling quickly, pouring out a list of the things that were most precious to her. The memories came piling in like the thawing of a frozen river, clinking with ice and pain: my mobile, my violin, my books, music, Horace the red velvet horse. Toothpaste. Toast and Marmite. She put her notebook aside; exhausted, relieved.

She rummaged through the store chest for something to

read, and found a school exercise book with George's name on the front. She looked idly through it, smiling to herself. It seemed to be mostly a series of charts and graphs where he had been recording heights of tides, sightings of birds, weather patterns, names of clouds, over several years of visits to the island. The early ones were very neat, and she imagined the earnest little boy that he must have been; face screwed up in concentration, hair flopping over one eye as he wrote. Later, the writing became more of a scrawl of scientific facts, mostly indecipherable. She looked at a list on one page, which named the terms of something called the Beaufort scale, describing conditions of the wind on a scale of one to twelve, from calm to hurricane. The list started with 'mirror calm', when the sea was completely flat. She tried to decide where today's sea would be on the scale. How about number 4? 'Moderate breeze. Small waves. Some white horses.' How poetic, to have words like mirror calm and white horses on an official list. It meant that the elements couldn't be described in technical language. She liked that idea. George's father probably liked that, too. She spoke aloud the words that named winds: sirocco, tornado, tempest, whirlwind, hurricane. Whoever thought of such beautiful words for such devastating winds?

She put the book down, too restless to try to absorb any

more information. If the tide was high by now, and someone had seen her flag, her rescuer would be on his way. She should be there to greet him. But where should she stand? Maybe the best place would be Landlook Point; she would see him coming, and wave and shout and cheer him on his way. She could dance like the selkie.

The light was already slipping fast. Surely it wasn't evening yet? She was confused. The blue of the sky was so pale that it was almost colourless, drained to water. The yellow sun stained the sea with swirls of amber. The tide was not full, but whether it was coming in or going out she had no idea, she had lost count of time and tides, days and nights. Maybe she had miscalculated it after all; and she had missed high tide altogether. She had no idea now. All she knew was the route she took to cross the island, familiar to her now as the route to school or town at home. She trod the path that had been trodden for hundreds and hundreds of years by monks and miners, crofters and fishermen, keepers of the lighthouse, from point to point and cove to cove, a tight web of patterns woven into the island's bones.

The tide was at ebb or flood, she decided. Which? What time was it? Anyway, the sandbank was exposed. It was a dark streak across the yellow gleam of the sea. And now, like yesterday, she could make out that something was standing at one end of it. A post? A tree? Could that be possible? Maybe it was a high tide marker? It was the wrong shape for a buoy, too upright, too long and thin. But she hadn't noticed it at any other time before yesterday. That was strange. George had pointed out the sandbank and told her how dangerous it was. They had looked at it for a long time. Surely she would have seen the post or whatever it was then. But yes, there was definitely something there. She realised that she still had the binoculars round her neck. Her hands were shaking as she turned the whorled wheel and put the binoculars to her eyes. Slowly, slowly, the figure of a person emerged. Deep inside her, she had known it would. Someone was standing there, face turned towards the island. Who was it? A man? A boy? Slowly, slowly, like an image in a dream, the person lifted his arm and waved.

'George! George! I can see you!' she shouted, uselessly pitting her voice against the knowing laughter of the gulls that were streaming round her in a sudden frenzy of play. She scrambled down to the Lone Lassie's stones and called again, waving both her arms in the air. He was coming across to her. Her exile was over.

'George!'

'The boy will never make it to the island.'

Ellie swung round, startled by a voice behind her. A young woman, not much older than herself, was standing close to her on the stones, wrapped in a long grey coat that clung damply round her ankles. Her long wisping hair was lifting and settling around her; the only thing that moved. She was gazing beyond Ellie towards the distant bank.

'How do you know?' Ellie gasped. Her voice was a cold, dry thing trapped in her throat. Who on earth was this girl, and how had she got to Wild Island, and why was she standing staring out to sea as if she couldn't really see Ellie at all, only what was beyond her; the figure on the sandbank?

The girl just shook her head and drove her hands deep into her pockets.

'Never.' There was such a sigh to her voice that it was hardly to be heard at all. 'He'll never come.'

'He will.' Ellie was frantic with fear and dread. 'He's going to save me. He's going to take me away from the island.' She turned and held the binoculars up to her eyes again. But the light had dropped, the sea-mist had risen, and the figure on the sandbank had disappeared from sight. And when Ellie lowered the binoculars and turned back, the girl with the long hair had vanished too.

CHAPTER SIXTEEN

When, three days earlier, George had sailed *Sprite* to Kyle to buy supplies and heard his father's frightening news about Morag, he had run straight to the railway station to find the time of the next train to Glasgow.

'In thirty minutes,' the bored man in the ticket office told him. 'And that's the last today, so you're lucky.'

George calculated rapidly. He would be in Glasgow soon after ten that night; he could get a taxi straight to the hospital. He might be in time. *Please, God, let me be in time. Don't let her die. It's unthinkable. Don't let Morag die.*

With shaking fingers he counted out some money and pushed it across the counter. Thirty minutes to wait. Thirty minutes!

Then he remembered Ellie. There was no time to go back to the island for her. He had to let her know what had happened. He had no idea what he should do. Somehow he must get a message to Guthrie to bring her back to Kyle, but then what would she do? She couldn't even go to Izzie's house, because his aunt was in Glasgow now. He counted out the rest of his money. Plenty. There was enough for Ellie to buy a ticket home. Then she'd have to go back to her house, fend for herself, phone her mother or one of her friends; whatever. At least she'd be off the island, not on this tide, but surely on the next.

'Have you got an envelope?' he asked the ticket man. 'Please?'

Unwillingly, recognising the boy's panic, the man tipped himself off his stool and rummaged through a drawer behind him, found an envelope and shoved it across the counter.

'And a pen?' George begged. 'Sorry.'

He pushed all the money he had left into the envelope, sealed it, and scrawled across it. *Morag very ill. Please bring Ellie over. Give her this money to get home. George.* His hands were shaking so much that the writing was barely legible. He rolled the pen back over the counter, careered out of the station, leapt over a dog's lead and nearly collided with the children's miniature bus. There was no sign of Guthrie, of course. The fishing boats were all out. He knew that Guthrie lived in one of the white cottages down by the front, but which one? At one time they had all been fishermen's cottages, but most of them were holiday lets now. Which one, oh which one, he moaned. Then he remembered that Guthrie had a black cat, Captain. Sure enough, Captain was sprawled across the windowsill of one of the cottages, snoozing in the late sunshine. Thank you, Captain. George stroked the cat, pushed the envelope through the letterbox in the door of the cottage and hurled himself back to the station. The train was in, trembling for take-off. George charged onto the platform and flung himself through the last open carriage door. He sank into a seat and closed his eyes. *Be in time! Let me be in time!*

At the fishermen's cottages, the sun had moved. Captain poured himself off the windowsill of the vacant holiday let and strolled next door to Guthrie's cottage. He eased himself in through the cat-flap.

CHAPTER SEVENTEEN

The wind was delving into Ellie's hair, snatching her breath away, sending a fizz of sand against her face. Green and grey waves frisked around Lone Lassie's stones. Ellie knew that the sandbank would be covered in moments. Crashing waves reared now against the rocks of the island. She imagined her seals plunging deep into them, nosing through the churning foam into the black, calmer waters of the deep ocean. She imagined the figure on the sandbank, lost in the rushing tide.

At last she pulled herself away from the rocks. It wasn't safe to be there any longer. None of that was real, she told herself. There was never anybody there, on the sandbank. There was never anybody on the rocks. *But she spoke to me.* It was all in your head; it was your own voice speaking. It must have been. Let it go. You are going mad with loneliness. Don't let it happen; think of something real. *They were ghosts.* Sinuous as fishes, the thoughts slipped back, and again she tried to drive them away. *This island is haunted.* Think of solid things. Houses. Buses. Books. Head down into the wind, she climbed away from Landlook Point, and when she paused to catch her breath again she saw a blue boat close to the island. It was Guthrie's; surely it was Guthrie's. Her rescuer had come.

She lost sight of the boat as she scrambled over the rocks and veered off the main path towards the shell beach, where a few days earlier *Miss Tweedie* had brought her and George in to land. She slithered down, careless of her footing, sending small stones skittering away from under her feet. The rapidly freshening wind brought rain with it now, and the rocks were wet and slippery. She was stumbling straight into the squall. Cold rain lashed into her, plastering her hair to her cheeks like wet seaweed; coursing down her neck and squelching round her feet.

She paused for breath a few metres from the cove, looking down into it. She could see Guthrie's boat clearly now. It seemed to be in some difficulty, because surely it was heading in the wrong direction. She ran down to the shore, skidding and slipping, yelling now, waving her arms frantically as the boat lunged and lumbered through the great swollen waves that seemed to have risen from nowhere; that seemed intent on swallowing her rescuer whole. In utter, helpless dismay she watched as at last Guthrie and his boat lumbered away up the east coast of the island towards Cormorant Cliff and disappeared into the mist of spray. It must be too rough for him, she told herself. He was in danger of smashing against the rocks. There was nowhere else around the island where it would be possible for Guthrie to bring in his big fishing boat; all the creeks and coves were too narrow or too shallow. He had tried to rescue her. And he had failed. She was still alone. Forlorn, she made her way back up to the cottage.

The door was closed. She had to kick it to open it, and it took all her strength to do it. There was a plastic crate on the kitchen table, filled with food. There was a scribbled note next to it, and she snatched it up eagerly. The light was dim, but she could just make out the words. The message was printed in a shaky hand that was unused to writing. *George. Molly asked me to bring your supplies over for you, as you forgot to collect them the other day. Looked for you but couldn't find you. Cannot stop because bad weather on way. Take heed. Take care. G.*

Ellie sank down into the chair and cried. She held the note balled up in her hand, cradling it as if it was her last link with home. She had tried so hard to be brave and positive, because it was what her father would have wanted; it was what her mother would have hoped. And now, after all that, to have come so near to her rescuer and to have missed him, was beyond bearing. Rain battered against the tin roof of the kitchen; loud and insistent and triumphant. The wind howled around the cottage. And the sea, the crashing angry sea, seemed to pulse with her own coursing blood, seemed to be part of her.

She was shivering now with cold and fear and utter loneliness. Rain streamed against the window. All the world was water; the sky, the dripping grass, the sodden earth; all water, nothing else. Eventually she stumbled into the living room and climbed inside George's sleeping bag, pulled it up around her face, and gave way to despair.

It was hunger, in the end, that made her crawl out of her bed at last. She searched through the contents of the crate that Guthrie had brought for her. Milk, bread, butter, jam, cheese, some sliced meat, potatoes, onions, carrots, cabbage, biscuits, marmalade, porridge oats. Batteries for the torch. Beer. Chocolate. And now, the sight of all this food that she had fantasised about for so long made her feel more wretched than ever. So George had been to Molly's shop all those days ago, as he had said he would. He had ordered beer and chocolate, their treats. And then he had just gone away somewhere and left her without them. Why? Why? Guthrie obviously thought George had come back to the island. What had happened to him? She thought of the figure on the sandbank; she thought of the ghost-girl on the steps. 'George, George,' she moaned. 'What has happened to you?'

She ate some cheese and bread mechanically, but the food made her feel better. The wind seemed to have abated a little, probably with the turning of the tide. The rain was pouring steadily, but not gusting as it had been. She tried to do some painting; something real, to steady herself, to bring her back to normality, to help her think of home and comfort and safety. She arranged a bowl of fruit and vegetables from the crate, beautiful colours gleaming in the candlelight. Her painting was mechanical too; it had no heart in it. All she could think about now was the boy on the sandbank. She opened up other colours, she mixed grey and brown and green, she swirled them onto the page; waves, crashing round a sandbank. In the centre, a black figure. She tore the page out of the sketchbook, screwed it up, flung it into the waste bag. She picked up a book to read, put it down again; walked through to her bedroom, walked back, sat on the chair with her hands over her face. *It's not just George*, she thought. *It's Morag, and Mr Donaldson. Why have they abandoned me here?*

Why doesn't somebody come for me? She stood up again and paced aimlessly round the little room. *Do something. Don't just wait for someone to come and rescue you. Do something.*

She was too restless to stay in the cottage. She decided to go and check on her flag. Surely Guthrie should have seen it? If he hadn't, then she had put it in the wrong place. She wore the huge wellingtons and heavy waterproofs that were hanging by the door. 'No wonder they keep these here,' she said aloud, and was surprised by the sound of her voice, querulous and young. 'No escape from the weather on this island.' She pulled the hood over her hair and ploughed back to the little beach where she had left the flag. Light was low now; evening was really here. Soon it would be full dark because the sky was so overcast. There would be no moon or stars tonight. Fool that she was, she had forgotten to bring a torch, even though she had fitted in the new batteries. She wouldn't stay long.

And there was no need to. The stake had been washed away. Her flag was a damp, torn rag floating in a rock pool. She waded out to it and scooped it up, wrung it out, and draped it over a rock above the tide line. It would never be seen from the sea now. Maybe a helicopter would spot it one day if someone was flying over the island looking for her.

Think, think, she told herself. Don't despair. What next? She would have to think of another plan. Maybe she could use the white bone shells she had found in that cave to write out the word 'HELP' or 'SOS' – up on the summit of the Height perhaps, that would be a decent spot. Maybe a helicopter could even land there. But not tonight. It was too late, growing too dark already; it would be a morning's work tomorrow. Ellie looked at the driftwood she had piled up, scattered now by the tide and the wind. The wood was soaked through. Tomorrow, tomorrow, she would carry it up from the beach, and when it was dark, she would light a bonfire.

The sky grew dimmer; the darkness of the sea grew deeper. She walked slowly, hands deep in her pockets, back up the path and out onto the summit of the Height. She could just see the heaving circle of sea on all sides, wherever she looked; imprisoning her. Long ago, George had told her, a king was exiled here. How lonely he must have felt, in his tiny, locked-in kingdom of Wild Island. She crouched down so she was kneeling on the wet grass, face upturned to the sky, letting the rain wash over her. The moon was barely out, hazily peering through the rainclouds. She felt too desolate to go back to the cottage. Take me home, someone. I don't want another night alone. Please. Please. Take me home.

Now she was aware of another sound. It was not the sweep of the rain across the grass, or the restless crashing of the waves on the rocks. It was not the high, desolate sobbing that gulls make, or the guttural call of the cormorant. It was a human voice, a young woman's voice. It was coming from the direction of the lighthouse.

It was the sound of someone singing.

CHAPTER EIGHTEEN

Dad. I'm going to paint the lighthouse for you. I'm in the cottage, looking out of the bedroom window at the back, where I never go. There's a fireplace in there, and I've lit a small smoky fire with the knuckles of driftwood that I brought in yesterday. I have a mug of hot chocolate on the hearth.

I have just woken up, and the storm has passed. I feel calm and rested. I don't know how I managed to sleep. I should be screaming. I should have dissolved into madness. I don't understand why I have not. I have been abandoned on a little rock of an island, and it is haunted. A girl lives here. I have seen her. I have felt her presence. I have heard her speak. I think she lit the fire for me the other night. I don't know how.

And last night, she sang. But she is not alive. She is a ghost.

So. I will paint the lighthouse, to show you that I am not going mad. I will cover the page with deep blue, ice blue. I think it is very early morning, unless it's already evening – but could I have slept that long? Anyway, now the clouds are clearing to show a few last stars, or early stars. I will paint them in. And there is the lighthouse, like a bright white candle. It is very beautiful in this after-storm light. Is the girl up there, on the gallery, watching? I will paint it now. It is a beautiful thing to see, and it is for you.

When she had finished the painting, Ellie put it to dry by the window and washed her brushes. She stood back to look at the painting. It was very calm, almost a holiday picture. There was nothing menacing about that lighthouse at all; nothing to alarm her. She decided that she would get to know it; would explore it. In full daylight there could be nothing to frighten her there. Later, she would do the things she had promised herself; collect the white stones and shells, write the SOS, pile up the driftwood to make a fire. But at the moment all she wanted to do was to see the lighthouse. The more she looked at her painting, the more inexorably drawn to it she was. She had to go there. Now.

The metal door to the lighthouse opened easily. As she stepped inside, it swung to behind her, slamming with a clang that echoed round the walls. Light from the high portals glowed softly down, illuminating the inside of the tower with a ghostly glow. She felt she was in a hallowed place, like a cathedral; lofty, dim and echoey. A huge metal shank thrust right up the centre of the tower from the ground floor to the lantern room at the very top. A wrought-iron spiral staircase wound its way round the inner wall, like an ammonite. She mounted the steps slowly, clutching her torch in one hand, grasping the stair rail with the other. When she reached the first of the tiny portals she paused for breath and peered out at the grey, endless ocean.

There were three storeys to the lighthouse. At each level the spiral stairway spread out into a platform that she could step onto and walk round. Ellie carried on up past the first and the second and finally into the very top space, the lantern room, which was completely surrounded by windows. There was no lantern there, no slats of glass or mirrors, no sign that there was anything that could have made or reflected light. She remembered going to the working lighthouse with her father, not long ago. They climbed up the spiral staircase, puffing and laughing, counting each step. They watched the mirror blades of glass that was called the lantern twist and turn, catching light, throwing it out, making rainbows of one another. The machinery glided silently round on a bed of mercury. Her father had told her about Fresnel, who created a new type of lens that was used in lighthouses. He told her about Pharos in Alexandria, the first lighthouse ever, and that it was one of the Seven Wonders of the World, and he told her about Stephenson who built many of the lighthouses in Scotland, on lonely islands and rocks in the sea. No wonder his son wrote *Treasure Island*, he had said, and he had started to tell her the story of Jim Hawkins and the pirate Long John Silver. She remembered all that as if he was there with her now. She could hear his voice, the huskiness of it when he spoke to her softly like that, in the storytelling voice of her childhood. She had walked with him up that staircase, and she heard him telling her not to look down till they got to the top, and when she did, she had seen the staircase opening below her like a huge throat gaping to swallow her up.

Now she saw a door leading out onto a gallery, and she went through it, touching the rail with her hand, walking round the whole circumference of the outside of the lantern room, enjoying the wild giddying sense of space and the huge, uninterrupted panorama of sea, sea, sea. She spread out her arms; at one with the fulmars and gulls that swooped round her; a girl of the clouds, a girl of the sky, a girl of air. She could see fishing boats like crouching birds on the sea, cargo boats on the horizon, small white-sailed yachts near the shore. 'I'm here! I'm here!' she called. 'Look at me! Look at me!'

At last she went back into the lighthouse, closed the door to the gallery firmly behind her, and wound her way down to the second platform. *This must have been an office*, she thought. There were a couple of stools, some framed charts, and a polished wooden writing table, neatly fashioned to curve into the rounded wall, and with an inkwell set into it. On each side of the desk there were two curved drawers. The brass handles were peculiarly carved in the shape of hands. She reached out to one of them gingerly, almost expecting the hand to open out, fleshy and cold, and grasp her own. She felt furtive and guilty, like an intruder; her heart was pounding. There was a silence of waiting around her, as if the lighthouse itself was holding its breath, as if someone was watching her.

The carved handle was warm to touch, and, encouraged, Ellie grasped it gently. It lifted up on a tight hinge to reveal a keyhole, but the drawer didn't budge. She tried the other drawer. It slid open easily, and was empty. Intrigued now, she tried the first one again, tried twisting the handle, knelt on the floorboards and felt underneath to see if it was caught in any way. No, it was definitely locked, and the key was missing, probably lost years ago. She stood up, dizzy from groping under the desk; faint even, cold and sweating now, her head throbbing, her heart hammering, her limbs weightless. She felt as if she was not alone in the room, as if someone else was there, breathing the air, taking air into itself, taking it from Ellie. She swayed and lost consciousness.

She opened her eyes to find herself lying face down on the floor. The sense of another presence had gone; the air was clear, she could breathe again. She had no idea what had happened, but what she did know, with absolute certainty as if the knowledge had been whispered into her brain while she was unconscious, was that the drawer was no longer locked.

She stood up slowly and grasped the handle. As she edged open the drawer she heard something rolling; something heavier sliding. She pushed her hand inside and drew out a wooden pen with a metal nib, and a black notebook. She opened the book, puzzling over it to decipher the unfamiliar, old-fashioned script; the slanted handwriting of a different age. Even when she focussed the torch on it, it was nearly impossible to read properly. She pulled a wooden stool across to the desk. It scraped the floor with a sudden screech, like a woman's high-pitched voice. She perched herself on it, leaning with her elbows on the desk, carefully studying the words; slowly turning page after yellow page. Finally she made out that it was a lighthouse keeper's log from over two hundred years ago, and that it covered a period of nearly seventy years. She eased herself up, stretching her back, and as she did so she heard the creak of the lighthouse door below her being slowly opened, and then slamming shut again.

'The wind,' she told herself, breath held tight, ears strained.

Now she could hear the lightly ringing tread of someone slowly and steadily climbing up the stairs.

CHAPTER NINETEEN

The hospital family waiting room was bare except for half a dozen blue-seated chairs and a machine for making coffee and tea. There was a rack of pamphlets on the wall: 'Living with Alzheimer's', 'Help for Carers', 'Smoking can Kill'. George was leafing through them, reading them one after the other, not absorbing a single word. The letters bobbed like tadpoles on the page. His father sat with his legs apart and his forearms resting on his thighs, hands clasped, head bowed. His mother was sitting upright in her chair, eyes closed, face tight and drawn. Her sister-in-law, Izzie, was clasping her hand in her own. Nobody spoke. Nobody had said a word since the staff-nurse had asked them to leave the Intensive Care Ward where Morag was lying under deep sedation. All four started when the door of the waiting room opened. George stuffed a leaflet on 'Palliative Care' back into the rack. Bill stood up, hands dangling at his sides now. His wife whimpered and leaned against Izzie's shoulder. Outside in the corridor, a painter whistled as he dabbed white gloss on the window frame.

Instead of growing louder, the footsteps grew fainter until they faded away and stopped. Ellie stayed as still as stone, the logbook fully opened in front of her, her eyes fixed on the stairs winding up from the floor below and on up to the lantern room above. Her heart was hammering.

'Who is it?' she whispered. 'Who's there?' Her voice flittered like moth wings into the silence.

Was there somebody standing on the stairs below, poised, listening too, staring up to see who had spoken? Had they turned and crept back down the staircase and out into the safe daylight? Ellie waited until she could bear it no longer. She groped the torchlight round the room. She went to the stair rail and shone the torch down the winding stairwell, round and round, until it caught up with a shadow thrown against the curved wall. It was the shape of a young woman, loose-haired, long-coated, stilled in a pose of watching and listening. Could it be the girl who had stood on Lone Lassie's steps? Ellie stared at it, unable to move, unable to swing the beam of the torch to make it light on the maker of the shadow, the ghost-girl. How can a torch light up a shadow?

Does a ghost *have* a shadow, does a ghost make footsteps, can a ghost speak? she asked herself wildly. Is she real? Who is she? Who are you? But she couldn't make her voice say the words, she could do nothing but keep her torchlight on the shadow, until it slowly faded away to nothing at all.

Ellie scrambled down the stairs, clutching the book in one hand and the torch in the other. When she was halfway, the book jerked in her hand as if was being snatched away from her. As she tried to clutch it back it fell to the floor and rolled down the stairs, pages fluttering like panicking wings. Ellie ran after it and stepped over it, too scared to pick it back up. Sobbing with fright, she pushed the door open and stumbled out of the lighthouse.

Chapter Twenty

*Dad. I am not writing now about a painting that I am about
to do. I am writing about the painting I did last (was it just
this morning, a few hours ago?) – the view of the lighthouse
from the back window of the cottage. It was finished.*

Ellie paused. Her writing was a scribble across the page.
He wouldn't be able to read it. No-one would be able to read
it, not even she, if she didn't control herself. But she couldn't;
her hands wouldn't stop shaking, and the words scribbled
out from her pen like ants scurrying across the page. She
couldn't stop writing. It was as if she was actually speaking
to her father, blurting out her story between sobs and gasps.
She couldn't stop now.

*I've just come back from the lighthouse. I thought I
was all right, Dad. I'm not. I'm going mad with loneliness,
with fear that I'll never be rescued, with anger at George for
leaving me here (Would he? On purpose? If not, where is*

he? What's happened to him? What's happened to Morag and their parents?); I'm weary with utter, utter helplessness and hopelessness. Only my painting and my notes to you keep me in touch with my SELF, with reality.

I keep hearing voices, sighs, whispers, footsteps. I see shadows where there is no body. I hear singing that doesn't exist from a lighthouse that no-one uses any more.

That's why I wanted to paint it for you, so you would know, if I ever escape from here, what I have seen.

And if I don't escape from here, if I die here – because now I can write these words, I can throw these thoughts into the air like scary birds – you will know what I have experienced. She paused, and looked up. Yes. It's true. I might die here. A cold white terror swept over her, dizzying her. Her eyes were burning with tears. I might. Die.

Write, write, write.

I love you, Dad.

Oh, I have food, plenty now. I have shelter. I should be fine. But for how long?

And I have fear, and it might choke me.

I'm trying to be brave.

I'm trying so hard.

THE COMPANY OF GHOSTS

I'm trying to tell myself that all these weird happenings are just my over-tired, helpless imagination playing tricks on me. Of course the island isn't haunted. How can it be? There are no such things as ghosts.

Because, after all, there's been nothing physical to frighten me. The sounds I hear could be tricks of the sea, of the wind, of the mice, of the birds. The lights and shadows I see, the figures slipping in and out of vision, the girl, the boy on the sandbank, they could be tricks of moonlight, starlight, candle-light, firelight. I know that. I keep telling myself that. But who lit the fire in the cottage? Maybe Guthrie had called in that day too, and not left a note. Maybe George did come back for me, and lit the fire, and went away again. Yet next morning the fire had burnt itself out completely. There were no ashes. How could that happen? Had I imagined the fire, because I was so tired, because I was in so much need of comfort?

But now I have solid proof that there is somebody else on this island. I have not imagined it. Someone lives here, but she isn't a ghost. She lives here.

I told you I had left the painting of the lighthouse to dry. It was finished. It showed the lighthouse in sunshine, on a beautiful day, as it had been the first time I saw it.

181

A lighthouse with no light, just as I have seen it now; a shell with no bright eye. When I had finished painting it, I fastened the lids on all my tubes of paint, as you've always told me to do, so they don't dry up. I emptied the mug of water, so I wouldn't knock it over and spoil my painting. I washed and dried my brushes, so the paint wouldn't dry on them and spoil their smoothness. I did all that, because that is what you have taught me to do and I always do it.

But just now, the first thing I saw when I came into the cottage was that the table was littered with tubes of paint, all opened. The mug was scummy with dirty brown paint water. My brushes were clumped with dried-up gunge, and the hairs splayed out like chimney-sweep's brushes.

And someone had spoiled my painting.

You will see that it's not my style, my neat observant style. The light has been put in, pouring out from the lantern room at the top, but it's an ugly, jagged line of white, streaking and turmoiled. The whole painting is boiling and frothing as if a wild sea is crashing over it, huge transparent waves, great plumes of white spray, and wild, whirling flourishes of black and brown and deep dark green. I could never paint like that. It's as if the painter was in a frenzy, flinging splinters and splashes of colour in every direction.

Or was it me, in the middle of a nightmare?

Ellie pushed the sketchbook away, feeling weary, feeling better, and looked up. Sitting in the chair facing her at the other side of the table was a girl, the same girl, surely, a young woman of eighteen or so. Her hair fell in long, curling strands about her shoulders; her eyes were huge and dark and unbelievably sad.

'So you do exist,' Ellie whispered. Her voice was trembling. Her whole body was trembling; cold.

'I live here.'

'Where? This house? The lighthouse? The old boat?'

'Here.'

Ellie tried to cling on to reality. Was she speaking to herself? Was she seeing nothing but dreams?

'Was it you I heard singing?'

Oh nothing, nothing. Talk to me, talk to me please. But why hadn't George mentioned her? *You are real. I want you to be real.*

If the girl lived on the island, then she was not alone. She need not be afraid. This girl was no ghost. She was real enough to touch. And yet Ellie was too afraid to do that, to reach out and touch the pale hand that was resting on the table. And why was she trembling, if she was not afraid?

Why was she cold and faint with fear? Why did her dry tongue stick to her mouth, and her voice break into pieces, and her breath come sharp and jagged as broken glass? *I am not afraid*, Ellie told herself.

'Who are you? Please tell me.'

The girl stood up. Her hair tumbled like falling leaves around her shoulders. She faded into nothing. Nothing.

Dad. All I can do is paint and write and walk. I can't eat or sleep, I can't change my clothes or wash myself or comb my hair. I go from the slipway to Cormorant Cliff to Landlook Point and back again and back again. I hear that tune, all the time. Sometimes it is sweet and lilting and dancing, and sometimes it is so slow and mournful that it would break your heart to hear it. I can't get it out of my mind, so I don't know any more whether I'm really hearing it, really hearing someone singing it, or whether it's just in my head.

Ellie remembered she had promised herself that she would make an SOS of white shells and stones to be seen from the air. At least it would be something to do. She worked at it as slowly as she could, to fill the time, ekeing out minutes, stretching seconds.

She went from cove to cove collecting shells, and up to the Height, and back again, struggling against a wind that was splintered with rain. She thought about white horses carved into the hillside, primitive works of art. Maybe she could make a picture out of shells, after she had finished her message. She would leave something beautiful there. Oh! A wonderful idea! She would make a picture of *Sprite* out of shells, just as someone had made a picture of *Spectre* on the hidden slate in the cottage. But what was the point? No-one would see it except the great flapping screaming gulls. They would squint down at it and mock it with their screeching laughter. She stood up from her task, stretched her arms out, and turned a full, slow circle. There was nothing on the ocean, except storm. All she could see was the endless roll of it, the plunge of it, the way it shook its wild white hair. No boats. No sandbank.

She wondered where the girl was, and whether she was watching her, walking with her wherever she went. And why does she watch the sandbank? What does she know? Is the figure on the sandbank a boy? A ghost? Is it George? Is it his ghost? Is he drowned?

No, I must not think like that. Paint, walk, read. Don't think.

Dad. I have done more paintings for you. They are all of

the sea in different lights – pale dawn light, sunlight, dusk, rain, moonlight. The light of a million stars in that black black black sky. Wild. Calm. I can't stop looking at the sea and I can't stop painting it. It is another person. It is master of this island. It is master of everything.

She closed up her sketchbook again, unable to concentrate. The only thing she could think about was the black notebook. She knew she had to go back to the lighthouse for it. Maybe it would tell her something about the mystery of this island.

'Do it. Do it now, Ellie,' she said aloud.

No. It's only a book. It's only a book. I can't go in there. I won't.

I'm afraid. I'm afraid of everything. I'm too frightened to go out of this door.

She walked round the cottage, too anxious to do anything; to sit, to eat, to draw. She had to learn to love the island again. Just days ago she had stepped willingly into Guthrie's boat, intrigued to come to the island; drawn to it. She had hated it when she first arrived, but George had shown her how to love it. She had to find a way of loving it again. She picked up her pencil and scribbled into the sketchbook

Ten things I like about Wild Island.

Nothing.

Think. Think.

1 *The bluey-purple mussel shells*

2 *The stars at night. Millions and millions*

3 *The curlews*

4 *That cave, the smugglers' cave, with its luminous green light across the water*

5 *The seals*

6 *The wild flowers*

7 *The blue throw on the armchair*

8 *George's sleeping bag*

9 *The food in the kitchen*

Ellie paused for a long time.

10 *The company of ghosts*

She reached out for her paints and brush. Her hands were firm; she was making quick sure strokes, black, white, black, black.

Shadows are everywhere now. I am surrounded by utter darkness – even in daylight, there is darkness around me. Even when there is no light at all, I am surrounded by shadows. Dad, I have painted shadows for you. Some are deeper than black. Some are sharp and defined, like silhouettes. Some flicker like leaves in sunlight. I have to paint them. You have told me that when I paint night scenes, I have to paint flat slabs of colour, planes with no shadings, no depth. I have done them for you. It calms me.

It makes me think of other things than fear. It makes me think of you and Mum. I think of us all sitting watching those old Lottie Reineger films that Nan bought on the Internet, those fairy tales told in silhouettes. When I saw them for the first time I only wanted to paint in black and white. We drew figures and Mum helped me to cut them out and make a shadow theatre.

So here are my shadows. Shadow gannets. Shadow lighthouse, shadow sailing boats, shadow shadows . . .

I want that black notebook.

I have to go back to the lighthouse for it.

Ellie put down her pen, put away her paints and cleaned the brushes and the mug. Now, she had to do it now.

But as she was about to go outside she saw her mother, clear as anything. She heard her voice: 'When did you last eat, Ellie Brockhole?' She frowned, holding onto the door handle. Was this real, or a dream, or a ghost, or a memory? She could see her mother in the beautiful clean kitchen of home, smiling round at her as she came down from hours painting in the studio that she and Dad shared, or revising for exams in her room.

Ellie said: 'I'll grab a sandwich.'

'No, you won't. Hot food is comforting. You need comfort, at your age. You work very hard.'

'I heard a man on the radio saying he'd never eaten a hot meal in his life,' Ellie remembered saying. 'And he was about forty, so it can't have done him any harm. No need to mess pans and create washing up.' She had smiled brightly, and her mother had ignored her and spooned hot stew onto her plate. 'There, my love. Eat.'

Oh, Mum. I'm so tired of pumping up water. I'm tired of opening tins. I'm tired of eating. I don't want to eat.

Guthrie had brought all that food, but she couldn't face it, couldn't bear the thought of actually cooking a meal.

Her mother's face was slipping away; she couldn't fix it in her mind; her mother's image had gone. Ellie broke down and cried.

'Oh, Mum. Mum. Please, please, please come and rescue me. I want to go home.'

'I want you to come home,' her mother's voice murmured, gentle in the air. 'Come back to me, Ellie.'

Ellie went wearily into the pantry at last and sorted through her lined-up tin soldiers. She opened a tin of soup, heated it on the little cooker, poured it into a mug, and stood on the doorstep of the kitchen, cupping her hands round it. She drank it slowly. Then she made up her mind. She put the mug carefully down on the step.

'Do it,' she said out loud. 'Do it now, before you lose your nerve. Do it, Ellie. Do it.'

'Ellie.' She thought she heard her name whispered behind her. Her skin prickled. She turned, but there was no-one there.

She left the cottage and walked slowly across the vivid, bouncing grass to the lighthouse. Tiny and sweet across the soft air came the sound of the girl's voice, singing. The same song, the same haunting tune that Ellie was always hearing. The door to the lighthouse was ajar. Maybe she had left it that way. She couldn't remember. She pushed it further and went in. It felt so cold in there. It was so silent. But the book wasn't there. She must go on. She had to find the book. She had expected to see it lying on the floor near the stairs, crack-spined from its fall from the floor above. She had expected to be able to snatch it up and run from the lighthouse with it.

Slowly, soundlessly, she climbed the spiral stairs. She could feel her breath fluttering in her throat; she was too frightened to set it free. Now she felt a flurry around her like a cold wind;

something made her flatten herself against the curved wall as if she was being pushed to one side as someone passed her. She listened, eyes wide, ears strained. Nothing, except for the rummaging of waves on rocks and the distant mockery of gulls. Every nerve in her body told her to turn and go back down the stairs and out of the lighthouse, and yet she carried on, past the portal with its glimpse of breathy mist, and up towards the platform where she had found the black notebook.

Now she could see a flickering yellow light that gave her a shadow to take with her. As she reached the platform she could see a candle glowing on the curved desk, casting into silhouette the dark shape of a girl with long hair curling over her shoulders. The girl was sitting at the desk, writing. Ellie froze and watched, breath pent inside her. The girl paused, pen poised, head cocked in thought. Then she dipped the nib of her pen into the ink well and began writing again. Like someone in a dream, Ellie absorbed the soft scratch of nib on paper, the moving hand, the shine of wet ink on the page; without questioning it, without trying any more to make sense of it. Eventually the writer stopped, blew gently on the page, and wafted the notebook lightly with her hand. Her stool screeched as she stood up and turned slowly towards Ellie, clasping the book.

As their eyes met, the girl's dark hair became grey, her firm skin grew loose and lined, and the pale hand turned veined and sinewy. The young sad eyes drew hanging flesh around themselves.

'Take the book, Ellie. It's yours now,' the old woman said. 'And when you have read it, I will tell you what you must do.'

Chapter Twenty-One

The consultant was a ruddy-faced man who looked as if he would be more at home working in the fields than in a hospital. He stood in the doorway of the waiting room and clapped both his hands together as if he was trying to wake the family out of a dream. George drew in a sharp breath. 'Please,' he whispered to himself.

'Morag is going to be fine now, fine,' the doctor said. 'We've taken her off sedation, and she's breathing normally, on her own, no tubes or oxygen mask.'

The sigh in the waiting room was like a thawing of ice.

'Thank you. Thank you, Doctor.'

George's father jumped forward and grasped the doctor's hand in both his own. His mother gave a gasp of relief and started to cry.

'It's been a bad time for you all, but Morag is through the worst and we're preparing to move her out of Intensive

Care and into the High Dependency Unit. We'll monitor her progress tonight and then hope to have her on the general ward tomorrow. And – back home by the weekend, I'm pretty sure of that.'

George went over to his mother and put his arm round her shoulders. She looked up at him, dazed.

'We still don't know what was wrong with her,' Izzie told him. 'Was it a brain haemorrhage, Doctor?'

'No, it wasn't. I have to admit that we don't know ourselves for sure what exactly has happened, but it seems to have been a very unpleasant and mysterious post-viral seizure. It gave us cause for serious concern for a while. But it's gone now, gone, I can promise you that, and all she needs is rest. We'll continue with blood tests, but everything is functioning normally again. There's no reason to think that it will ever happen again.'

Bill was still pumping the doctor's hand. 'You've been wonderful. You've all been wonderful.'

'It's our job, Mr Donaldson. I suggest you all take time off now. Morag is sleeping.'

'Sleep that knits up the ravelled sleeve of care,' Bill murmured.

The consultant rescued his hand and smiled at George's mother. 'Try to get some rest, eh?'

The family turned to each other, embracing one another, damp-eyed. They didn't even notice the doctor slipping out of the room to return to his work. Like people in a trance they collected together their bags and coats. George's mother slipped back into the ward and kissed her sleeping daughter gently. George stood with his father and Aunt Izzie, from the door, unwilling to risk waking Morag from her deep, natural, healing sleep. They gathered together again in the corridor and broke into animated chatter as they made their way to the coffee area.

'I feel I live here now,' Sheila said to George. 'I know all these women by name. I know how many grandchildren they've got and what they're going to be knitting next.' She was giggling with relief, pink-cheeked, bright-eyed; suddenly alert and in touch with her old chatty self.

'I think I'll go home for a couple of hours,' Bill said. 'Okay, Sheila?'

She shook her head. 'I'm staying here. I'm not going home till my girl speaks to me.'

'I'll stay with you for a bit,' Izzie told her. 'I'll get some drinks in now. But I'll catch the next train home and come back in a few days.'

'I can't take any more coffee. I'll bring you some fruit and stuff,' Bill promised. 'How about you, George? You could do with a shower, if you don't mind my saying. You've been wearing that T-shirt since you came off the island. And it's an out-of-date political statement anyway.'

'I'm kind of attached to it, Dad. Besides, I left my favourite one there.'

'A line of poetry would look better on it . . .'

'For Heaven's sake, Dad!'

'A nice bit of Tennyson – *In the touch of this bosom there worketh a spell . . .*'

'Stand in the shower and get rid of the smell.'

They were bantering together, sparring words as they always used to before Morag was taken ill. It felt good and natural.

'You should never have gone there in the first place,' his mother said. 'Your father told you to go straight to Izzie's.'

'Since when has he taken any notice of his father?' Bill groaned. 'He suddenly grew up and had a mind of his own.'

Izzie set a tray of coffees in front of them. 'This is just for starters. We haven't eaten properly for days. I've ordered cooked breakfasts.'

'We'll have to eat them ourselves,' Sheila said. 'They're off home.'

'I think I'll have that cooked breakfast first.' George grinned. 'I'm famished. I'll catch the bus, Dad.'

His father bent to kiss Sheila, softly, warmly, as though there was no-one else in the room, stroked her hair, and left them. Sheila smiled, watching him go, then turned dreamily to George.

'By the way. I've just thought. Have you heard anything from the girl?'

Chapter Twenty-Two

The lighthouse keeper's log began:

February 24ʰ, Eighteen hundred and twenty. I have just took over from my father, Dugald Hendry Monroe, deceased. At seven today my duties here began. I climbed the tower and put out the light. I drew down the curtains so the sun do not magnify the lenses and set on fire the house. No wind. Good light. Everything is well.

All my life have I lived here being born on this island in the year 1802 and I am now in my eighteenth year and my mother long dead. I have always known how to keep the light. With my father I used to check the lamp and polish the lenses daily. We would step out onto the gallery and wipe the windows clean. We were like birds then, high in the air and the weather. I know all things about the tides and the winds and the sun and the stars. Anabel is my name, which my father do think has the meaning of joy.

I do know the hazards of the sea. I have seen ships go down into the throat of waves. I have heard the wails of drowning men, and sometimes I do think the seals wail with the same voice. I have hauled shipwrecked sailors half-dead off the rocks and breathed life back into their bodies by the will of my own heart and the power of my own lungs. Yet last night my father did fall into the sea and not any part of me could save him. I cannot swim, and nor can he. I watched him go and now part of me is gone too. But though I do not hear his voice nor see his face no more, I have inside me his lovely knowings of the sea and I will do his work for him so help me God.

And I will not live here alone always because my bonnie sweetheart boy he vows to take me as his bride and Wiald Island will be his home too, and he being crofts man can make things grow and bring one cow across the water, hens and three or four sheep and we will live in love and peace. His name it is Adair but Boy I call him as his mother does. Boy he was when first we met and gave each other smiles and Boy I call him still for I love him so.

Octopus. Dead. The child Lachlan and his grandfather said they saw a pod of them when they were coming over to pick mussels yesterday.

Those were the first words that Ellie read in the black leather book.

Anabel Monroe. Born here in this cottage. So those were her initials carved into the fireplace. A M. And after her father died, and before her Adair came to live with her, she lived here on her own, like Ellie. But it was worse for Anabel. Her father had died. She *saw* him die. In eighteen hundred and twenty. Nearly two hundred years ago.

Now Ellie knew for sure that it was not out of madness or her imaginings that she had seen shadows and whispers and figures coming and going. The island *was* haunted, and the lighthouse, and the cottage. The ghost was Anabel, and she moved in and out of those places as if they were rooms of a house, as if space and time had no meaning for her. She had just that day written a final entry in the logbook. She knew Ellie's name; she had given Ellie the book. Perhaps, after all, she meant her no harm. Perhaps there was no need to be afraid.

She lives here with me. I live with a ghost; all the ghosts of Anabel, from girl to old woman. I have no other company here.

A sudden drumming sound startled Ellie out of her deep

reverie. It was raining; not the light drizzle that came with the sea-mist, but heavy driving rain that hammered on the tin roof of the kitchen and beat against the window like small bright pebbles. Yet through the little window she could see that the sky was an opalescent white, as if sunlight was trapped up there and leaking its light through the cloud cover. She took up a pencil and began to write, without pausing to think, as if she could hear Anabel's voice telling her what to say:

I know the skies – all the weathers it brings with its colours, the mists and the torrents. I know the white gleam of wet rocks and the sea like silver spread beyond it, and the white breath that rises up from it, as if the water is sighing.

Ellie stared at the words, whispering them to herself. She had heard the *heesh* of pen on paper, she had watched her hand moving. She touched the page lightly, as if her hand could make contact with the girl who had written there that morning. 'Anabel Monroe,' she whispered. 'Help me.'

And suddenly she felt calm; filled with hope. She was not alone. She went into the kitchen to make the curry she had promised herself. She chopped fresh vegetables. She found a tin of chick peas, a jar of curry paste, a packet of rice. 'Mum, how you would wrinkle up your nose at this! Curry paste from a jar!' She thought of her mother and herself working together in the kitchen, grinding coriander, cardamom and cumin seeds with the marble pestle, measuring out the lovely little pungent mounds of yellow and dun and brown powders, stirring them into a long slow bubble of rich simmering sauce; she imagined the amazing smells that pervaded the house on curry nights. 'You hate chick peas!' she said, smiling. 'They give you wind. Ah, but look at my rice! Perfect! Here you are, Mum. An instant curry. And, do you know what? It's delicious!'

'We could open a restaurant,' she remembered saying once. 'Dad could grow the veg, you could cook, and I could serve and get all the tips.'

Except Dad would never have succeeded with the vegetables. He wasn't in the slightest bit practical. He would stack them and arrange them and paint their beautiful colours, but a vegetable patch in his care would soon be a mess of weeds.

When she had eaten she curled up in the chair and tucked the blue throw around herself. She picked up the logbook again, flicking through the pages, hungry to read on; then turned back to the beginning. Beneath that first entry, in a scrawl that was barely legible, Anabel had written what seemed to be a secret message to herself:

I will not tell anyone about my father, when they bring supplies for me. I do not want other keepers to be sent to help me. I can keep watch all night to make sure the light stays lit. I know the night, I know the weight of it upon me and upon the sea. I can sleep by day. I can do all this. When Boy comes to marry me, he will be the new keeper. He will come to fetch me to be his bride, and then we will live here together always. And Boy can come this day. Low tide be twelve hour noon. I watch for him, heart full. I cannot row to him, for when the sea took my father's life it took the boat too. I will ask for another one day, and I will call the boat the same name. When Old Man Guthrie next brings supplies I will say, Specter is lost, but not my father. No.

Ellie paused in her reading. Guthrie. That was strange. Another Guthrie, from long ago.

When my father met Boy at Fish Green last Michaelmas they exchanged some things. It was my job to do that journey but this time Father said I must stay at home and he would row across. My father had crabs with him, and a bag of flounders still thrashing, and Boy had three chickens to give him in exchange. And Boy said, you have something else I wish for, Dugald Monroe, and his voice was soft and a blush was on his face, and my father said to him what do you give me in exchange, Boy Adair, and Boy said what do I need to give but all my life, and my father said you are still a boy and when time makes a man of you we will talk again. And you will not come to the island, my father said, until you are ready to be master of it. My father told me this when he came home with the chickens, and asked me if I knew what Boy had meant by this, and I said, no, Father, I don't. But I did.

Ellie closed the book, feeling that she was prying into someone's secret thoughts; none of it was her business. And yet the ghost girl-woman had given it to her. She meant her to have it. She wanted her to read it, surely. She opened the book again and flicked through the pages randomly:

Eleven am. Thick fog come down. Horn must blow. And then in Anabel's tight postscript scrawl: *How I do hate that sound, for it do mock my loneliness. How I do mourn and grieve upon its banshee wail.*

She read on, page after page of neat script, each day an entry about the state of the tide, the visibility, the wind, the weather, all in the precise manner of a log, and always, after the official entry, came a secret; a half legible scribble of private thoughts.

This low tide there was much salmon on the nets. If my father was here with his boat I would be taking them to Fish Green. Even though there are plenty nets out there off shore of Allan Bay, Boy would always take my salmon first and give me meat and eggs in exchange for them. I would swim to him if I could, I would swim in the sea like the hawks that do fly inside the water to catch their fish.

She's a bit like me, Ellie thought. She talks to herself, and writes it down. Maybe everybody talks to themselves when they're on their own. Maybe everybody does anyway. Maybe we all have a ghost other-self to have secret conversations with that nobody else hears. But what if you don't have any words to think with? How do babies think? The voice in my head never stops. It's like that rain on the roof, hammering and insistent. I'd like it to stop. I'd like my head to go quiet.

She glanced out of the window. The rain was easing, and the promised sun was peering through the spent clouds. She decided it was time now to gather up the driftwood she had collected and take it up the Height to make a bonfire. Maybe more wood had been washed up by now. She no longer felt frightened to leave the cottage. She had a name for her fear now, and it was Anabel. And Anabel was just a girl like herself; lonely. Happy with purpose, Ellie ran down and

205

started to collect up the various little piles of driftwood that she had squirreled away by the bone cave and in the little coves. Mostly it was very wet from the recent downpour, but she felt confident now that she would be able to light it, just as Dad had always managed to light the garden bonfire for Mum, even when it was wet with November rain. She hauled the sticks and logs up the Height, panting with effort, excited with energy. It was too early yet to light it. She went back to the cottage and finished off the cold curry, reading more of the log, this time from the middle section.

Light good, visibility good, wind fair but rising. I have trouble with the lantern light. The flame is black and sooty, and the lenses of the lantern do separate from each other. I have to keep the lantern lit all day and night because the pilot jet keeps going out. Some times I cannot manage on my own.

Old man Guthrie has brought a boat for me, with his grandson Lachlan rowing it. They have moored it in the creek for me. Specter, I will call it, like my father's boat. But the weather is too rough for me to use it yet.

This morning I did find a great skull upon the shore.

This day also a pod of whales did pass nearby. I see the fountains of water. I see the huge backs that do curve like great black round rocks. There is menace and fury in the sea.

And I am afraid of it.

I watch for Boy, and still he do not come.

And further on, in the same entry.

High tide brought strong winds, waves some thirty, forty foot. One Russian ship went down, and all hands lost. The boats came out from Kyle to save the men, and only found bodies washed against the salmon nets.

Sandbanks smothered all day long.

Ellie paused, and read the passage again. How could Anabel have written so calmly about that shipwreck and those lost lives, in the same space almost as the sightings of whales? She thought of the men wallowing in the waves, she thought of their shrieks and despairs, she thought of their wives and their girlfriends and their daughters waiting for them at home. Maybe there was no way of writing about such horror and terror and grief. Maybe in her long life of staring at the sea Anabel had seen such things so many times that all she could do was keep a record of it, like a bird-spotter ticking a list. And yet there were those words, dark with shudderings:

There is menace and fury in the sea.

And I am afraid of it.

She turned to the last but one entry. Compared to the earlier entries the writing was trailing and shaky, as if it had been written by an old, ill person. It was so difficult to read that Ellie had to take the book outside, though daylight was fading fast. One last read, and she would go and light the bonfire.

This day must be my last of service. I can no more climb the stairs from faintness, no more wind the clockwork. When I reach the ladder to the lantern room I have to haul my body up there like a sack of stones. I have no breath or strength to fight the weather now, nor do my eyes see as well as they might, not even when the gannet strikes the water; nor do my ears hear, not even the herring gull's mad screech. When Lachlan do come with my supplies, I will bid him do those tasks for me, and find another soul to take my place. But I will not leave this cottage while I live. I am waiting here for Boy.

The wind is soft. The sea lies calm. I trim the wicks. I leave the lantern safe. I will go down now to sleep. Amen.

The page was signed Anabel Monroe, and dated July 12th Eighteen hundred and eighty four. It was the last entry the old woman had made, until yesterday.

CHAPTER TWENTY-THREE

Ellie closed the book and sat quietly thinking. She felt calm again. She had not read all the entries, because they spanned over sixty years. She had skimmed through the book, picking out a page here, a page there. She felt she knew the writer, Anabel Monroe, as if she had met her face to face. *And I have*, she thought. *I have.* The log told her life-story, the daily simple happenings of a woman who lived on her own and who knew the sea and the sky and the weather as if they were her family. Maybe that final entry had been written on the day Anabel had died. So she had serviced the lighthouse on her own for over sixty years, and every day, it seemed, she had waited for Boy, watched out for him, longed for him. Ellie thought about the ghost figure on the Lone Lassie stones at Landlook Point, waiting, watching, longing still. She thought of the figure of the young man on the sandbank, hand lifted to wave, down all those years. How deep a love was this, that could never let go? And would Anabel always sadly haunt the rocks, the cliff, the sands and shores and stones on Wild Island, and never find peace?

Please, please, don't make me stay here till I die, Ellie thought, suddenly overwhelmed with the enormity of her own plight. One day the food in the kitchen would run out, and then what? Could she last out till her mother came home from her honeymoon? How long had she been there? She could no longer count the days and nights, merged as they were into sleeplessness and exhaustion. There was the night of the mice. The night after George left for Kyle. The night of the fog and the screaming horn. The night she painted the lighthouse. After that she was confused. Four nights – five? And the night she had spent at Morag's house. So she would have at least seven days more on the island before her mother came home. No-one would miss her till then. Panic rose up in her, fear quaking in her chest.

I can't last that long.

'Help me, Anabel.'

And out of the trembling stillness, a voice: 'Help *me*.'

'I don't know how to!' Ellie moaned. 'Leave me alone!'

All she wanted to think about was herself now, her own plight. When her mother finally came home, someone would set up a search for her, George would be questioned and would have to confess to his treachery. She wanted to go home, she wanted to lead a normal life again, to be with her mother and see her friends and wear new clothes. She wanted to have a boyfriend who would look something like George even though he had treated her so badly. But did he? Did he drown? She pushed the thought away; too painful to contemplate. She would rather think that he had tricked her than that he had died trying to come back to her. I've never even kissed a boy, not properly, she thought. Not passionately. Not with my heart full of love and hope and longing. Not to be his special person. *Never give all your heart*, the tile on the cottage bedroom mantelpiece read. But she wanted to do that, just that.

In Assembly one morning, Mrs Grieg had told them the Old Testament story of 'Jeptha's Daughter'. Jeptha had promised God that if he won a battle against the Ammonites, he would sacrifice the first person he saw on his return home. And it was his own child who came running to him to meet him. He told her he had to kill her, and she went up to the mountains to prepare herself; one last night with her friends. What did they talk about, Ellie wondered. Did they talk about the love that would never be for her, the children she would never have? Did she let sand trickle through her fingers and say that was her future, her life, trickling away? 'Don't don't don't think like that, Ellie,' she shouted. 'For heaven's sake, don't give in! Stop wallowing in self-pity. It won't get you anywhere!'

She ran to the kitchen, found the tin of matches and tore a few unused pages from her sketchbook. Then she climbed up to the Height to light her fire. It was not quite dark yet. Already the sky was pricked with early stars; soon they would blossom and flare in their millions. She crouched down and shoved screwed-up coils of paper into the cave she had left at the bottom of the bonfire. She had to waste half a dozen matches before finally an edge of paper caught fire. Black smoke puthered out at her. She blew into it to make the charred edge of the paper flare with flame again, and then squatted on her haunches, fanning the smoke that now came in curls of blue wisps. Bright yellow worms of fire wriggled between the kindling twigs, and then whooshed up, capering like frenzied dancers. She leapt back as the flames took hold. Now, now, her fire would blaze! The heat on her hand and her face was glorious. She danced round it; the beautiful light that ate up the sky and all the stars. 'Save me! Save me now!' she laughed.

But the fire was a hungry beast; it wolfed down every

stick she piled on it. Within half an hour there was nothing left but drifting golden sparks. The moon had risen, darkness was falling.

'Someone will have seen it! Someone, somewhere!' All she had to do was wait.

It was hard to decide where it would be best to wait. If her bonfire had been seen by a boat at sea, it would come round the back of the island, round Cormorant Cliff, past the creek, and onto the shore at the shell beach. It would make sense to wait at the shore. And yet if it had been seen at Kyle, then she could wait at Landlook Point and watch out for it, wave her torch, welcome it in. What if a boat came like Guthrie's had when he brought the supplies, and because he couldn't find her, didn't wait? Ah, but surely they would realise that the fire was a signal for help?

In the end she chose the shell beach below the cottage. The sea was running smooth and high now, gently lapping the rocks. Nothing could prevent a boat from landing there. She had chosen the perfect night to be rescued. The little waves glinted like millions of fish frisking against the rocks. Gallivanting, as her father would have said. Scallywagging, George had said.

'I can see you, wagging your scallies!' She smiled.

She remembered George's surprised laughter that morning at Cormorant Cliff, how he had smiled at her in a moment of shared fun; how close she had felt to him then, how warm in his company.

She watched the to and fro of the waves in the moonlight, mesmerised by them, the bow and curtsey of their perpetual dance. She was locked in a trance of waiting and watching. A cormorant screamed into the water and was swallowed into its blackness. The song of the ghost-girl pounded in her head, ceaseless, menacing, insistent, surging like the tide.

She finally gave up her vigil when morning came. She was cold and hungry. She went back to the cottage and made porridge, bread and jam, cocoa. She was almost too tired to eat. Afterwards, she curled herself up in George's sleeping bag. She found it easier to sleep at this time of day, when the frightening blackness of night had gone, when the sea birds were busy and the sun was warm. She slept heavily, and woke up refreshed. The warm light of day blessed her.

'I will not give up. I will not. I will not. Today I will start again. I'll find more driftwood. I'll find old clothes to burn, anything.'

And then an astonishing, daring thought came to her, so strong that it was as though someone had whispered the idea to her. She would not light another bonfire on that damp and windy hill, for it to blow out in minutes. She would light a fire in the lighthouse itself. It was so obvious!

She set out at once to search for more driftwood. There wasn't much, but she carried the few sticks and elbows and knotted branches she did find to the door of the lighthouse and piled them there, along with gulls' feathers and strands of black seaweed that had been cast up by the very high tides and dried themselves on rocks. Backwards and forward she went, intent on her task. 'This'll do, won't it? This'll burn all right,' she kept saying, and it was as if she was no longer talking to herself but to Anabel, who must be watching every move she made; her invisible shadow. Now she rummaged around for a container to burn everything in. It had to be small enough for her to carry and strong enough to contain a fire. Otherwise the wooden floor of the tower would catch light and go up in flames, like a magnificent rocket.

And then she remembered something that George had told her when they had been talking about the lighthouse. *There's a really old lantern at the back of one of the sheds – a proper lantern.* Maybe it was the very one that Anabel had used. It had to be. It would be the very thing to use. She went round to the tool shed that leant against the back of the cottage. Whenever she had tried to open the door before now it had refused to budge. The hinge had rusted and the handle had snapped off. The door had dropped and was leaning in, too heavy to be pulled or pushed in any direction. But today she was determined to get in. After ten minutes of desperate kicking and sweating she managed to break the door down. *Good firewood*, she noted. *If I need any after tonight*. She rummaged through a pile of mouldy folding beach-chairs, a musty tent, children's fishing nets, and there at the back, exactly as George had said, was the old lantern. It was badly rusted and one of the panes of glass was badly cracked, but it would do, it would surely do the job. She lumped it across the grass to the lighthouse and gradually managed to carry it up the staircase and to the tower ladder. 'I can do it, I can do it,' she told herself. 'I can do it because it will save my life.' She lifted the lantern up the ladder rung by rung, and then slid it across the floor of the lantern room.

She ran back down and carried up her armfuls of sticks and feathers and seaweed, her tin of matches. Everything was ready now for the beacon that would surely shine all night, and would be seen by ships at sea and people on shore, even though there were no lenses to magnify its light. She would polish the lantern and clean all the windows, like

Anabel had done. First she had to brush away the long trails of cobwebs that festooned them. Then she fetched water and a rag and washed the windows all the way round so they sparkled in the sunlight, inside and out. When she had finished she walked slowly round the outside gallery, trailing her hand along the railing. She looked out and down at the long blue shimmering stretch of ocean, at the ships on the horizon, at the tiny fishing boats with sails taut in the wind, at the white specks of seagulls on the water and in the sky, and last of all, she came to rest opposite the coastline of the mainland. She gazed at the white huddle of buildings that was Kyle, and beyond that, at the undulating blue mountains that led, far away, to home.

Now she must wait till nightfall. Her heart was jumping with anticipation and nervousness, and she couldn't settle to anything. There was a crackle like electricity in the atmosphere, a vibrant tension. The gulls were quiet, the sea was still. The light was strange. The sky was white, almost green. She wandered down to Seal Beach, her favourite, most magical place. There were no seals to be seen today. She had brought her rucksack with her, knowing that she couldn't go back to the cottage yet and spend all day there waiting. She would write to Dad and sketch something for him. It would be something beautiful this time, not the dark and troubled pictures she had done for him the day before. After all, there were many lovely things on the island; in the daytime, when the sun shone. And even in this strange light the island was beautiful. She pulled her sketchbook and paints out of her bag, looked round for an idea, and saw something that made her heart stand still as stone.

It was a curious, smooth, rounded shape, like a long, rolled body, and it was bleached to a very pale cream. It looked like a drowned body thrown up by the tide.

She put her things down and walked slowly up to it. Whatever it was, it was not a body. It was something that she had never seen on the beach before, although she had combed it time and again for driftwood. Maybe it had been brought up on the morning tide – and yet it was dry, dry and bleached as bone, and it had been dragged up higher than the high tide mark. How come she hadn't seen it before? And was it George's family who laid it here to rest? She paused. *When did that happen?* She wondered. When did Morag's family become George's family in her mind, as if he was the most important member – George who had deserted her, George her would-be murderer? She let that last thought go. It was too ridiculous. She let all the thoughts go. She remembered squatting by the hearth in the cottage, looking at the strange shapes of the driftwood he had collected.

'There's a really nice one that we've left on one of the beaches,' he had said. 'Where we found it. It just looks right there. We pulled it up above high tide line so it doesn't get washed away again.'

'You'll have to show me.'

'You'll have to find it.'

'Oh. Right.'

'It's better that way.'

And then she had accused him of watching her when she was painting the mussel shell. Anabel, it had been. Anabel had always been watching her.

The bulge at one end was like a head, and the knot holes in that head were like two eyes. She walked round it and looked at it from every angle, and then she realised what it looked like. It was a seal. The more she looked at it, the more seal-like it became, like the elephant rock that George had told her to find. It was a piece of driftwood, and yet now it could never be anything else but a seal.

Dad, I'm going to draw you something as beautiful as my seal, she wrote, *but it's not like drawing a real seal. I'm drawing something that looks like something real – like the ghosts of the island, like the shadows and the lights and the sounds; more dreams than reality. Nothing is real any more.*

She drew steadily, well into the evening. The sky slipped imperceptibly into grey and deeper grey, and eventually there was not enough light to draw by.

'It's time,' she said.

CHAPTER TWENTY-FOUR

'Ellie? Have you heard from her? I must get in touch with her mum. I expect she's gone down to her father's.'

George put his coffee mug down and stared at his mother.

'Did she have enough money with her?'

He scraped his memory. It seemed like weeks since he had left the island. When was it? Three, four days ago? To his dismay, he realised that he had hardly thought about Ellie since he had arrived at the hospital.

'She's fine. I asked Guthrie to bring her off the island. I left him a note and some money for her.'

'Hang on. Are you telling us that you left that girl on the island on her own? I thought you told me she'd gone back home?' His mother looked helplessly at Aunt Izzie. 'I haven't been in touch with her mother! Or have I? I can't think straight.'

George slumped back into the chair. He felt suddenly

wretched. Hesitantly, he told them about the sequence of events since he sailed into Kyle. He forced his brain to remember everything, mudded as it was with the trauma of the last few days, lack of food, too much caffeine, and the fug of hospital heat. He may have told them the story already, he couldn't remember. If he had, they couldn't remember, either. All they had thought about was Morag, hovering in a twilight world between life and death. Even now, Sheila had difficulty in following his story. She didn't want to have to think about it. She didn't want to think about anything except Morag's miraculous recovery. Slowly the connections were made, the strands plaited and tied.

'I can't handle this,' Sheila groaned. 'I don't want to. I don't even have her mother's phone number with me.'

'She'll be fine,' George said. His head was spinning. What if she wasn't? She must be, surely.

'Guthrie stays out in his boat overnight,' Aunt Izzie said. 'Even longer, sometimes. Isn't her mother away or something, George?'

'Yes. On her honeymoon.'

'So Ellie might be at home on her own.'

'I told you, she'll be fine,' George muttered. 'She's sixteen. She's not a kid.' He felt completely churned up. Surely, surely,

Ellie would be safe at home. She would simply have caught the train, like he had. It wasn't hard. She wasn't stupid. He thought of her running along the creek as he set off in *Sprite*, skinny and lovely and laughing, shouting out her request for a chocolate treat. Lovely. She was lovely. What had she thought when he didn't come back for her that night?

'I told her mother I'd look after her.' Sheila started rummaging into her bag. 'We'll have to phone Guthrie. At least we ought to check when she left the island.' She stared at George blankly. 'My God, what if she hasn't? What if that poor child is still there?'

George and Izzie watched her as she tapped out the number on her mobile. At the other end, the phone rang and rang into an empty house.

'Drat the man. Why on earth doesn't he get an answer phone?' She looked at them helplessly. 'George, as soon as you get home I want you to go to her house, okay?'

He shook his head. 'I've no idea where she lives, Mum.'

'We'll find out.' Aunt Izzie drummed her fingers on the table. 'What's her name?'

'Ellie.' George swung himself away from them, miserable now. He felt small and foolish and worried. Why, oh why, hadn't he tried to persuade her to come over to Kyle with him? He'd let her down; he'd just abandoned her and forgotten about her. But she'd be all right, surely?

'She'll be back home. She and her mum will have got in touch with each other. She might even have arranged to go on holiday with them after all.' He very much doubted that. Ellie had been so bitter and hurt when she talked about her mother.

'I'm sure you're right,' Sheila said, though privately she thought the same thing as George. Ellie and her mother had a lot of talking to do before they could heal the rift between them. 'I'm responsible for the child. She's in my care.' She drank her coffee slowly, remembering Ellie's tense, angry face that evening when Morag had brought her to the house instead of going to orchestra practice; and the difficult, uneasy telephone conversation she'd had with the girl's mother, and then in person. "We'll look after Ellie. Don't worry." Those were my last words to her mother. And what have we done? Deserted her, and left her to fend for herself.'

'You can hardly be blamed,' Izzie told her. 'In the circumstances, what else could anyone have done? What else could George have done?' She smiled at her nephew sympathetically. 'As he says, she's not a little girl. She's sixteen years old. Many a girl has left home by then. When we can speak to Morag we'll get Ellie's mobile number.'

'She won't know it. They hardly knew each other,' Sheila said. 'They weren't even friends. And I don't want Morag to know anything about this. I don't want her getting upset and worried. I've got her mother's number anyway, at home.'

'I'll go back now,' George said.

'It's in the notepad by the phone. But hang on – it's just the landline number, and she's away. Ellie was going to text me her mobile number, I remember now. Why didn't she?'

'She did try, when we arrived on the island,' George said. 'I'll phone that landline anyway. Ellie will be there, don't worry.' He was eager to go, but his mother grabbed his arm.

'If she's not there, look in the phone book. She might have gone to stay with relatives in town. It's a really unusual surname. Something to do with badgers.' Sheila frowned. 'Or vegetables. I know! Brockhole! You'll find that easily. Brockhole.'

But though George found the number readily, and phoned it several times there was never any answer from the Brockhole household. In the end he decided to go round to the house – he discovered from the phone book that Ellie lived in his part of town. His father had gone back to the hospital, so he had no car to drive. It didn't matter. He could be there in five minutes. He was happy at the thought of seeing her; sure now that she would be there. It was strange to see her house, the house of Ellie, a prim and neat semi. He wanted her to be in; wanted her to be standing in the window, watching him, pleasure and surprise lighting up her face as she ran to answer the door to him. But the house was in darkness; no-one was there. So where was she? In despair he knocked on the house next door. A boy of about his age answered.

'I wanted to speak to Ellie Brockhole. Have you seen her around?'

The boy leaned against the door-jamb. He liked Ellie too. He summed George up, aware of his eagerness. 'Might have.'

'Today, I mean. Yesterday – is she around?'

The boy shook his head. 'They're all away.'

'Together?'

'Sure. Some kind of family honeymoon.' The boy laughed. 'Sounds like fun.'

'If you see her – tell her George was asking.' George turned away, helpless.

'Okay.' The boy closed the door. 'As if,' he said.

CHAPTER TWENTY-FIVE

The shell sand beneath her feet crinkled, the little waves barely sighed, and total darkness fell. Ellie had to use her torch to light her way up the lighthouse tower steps. She had never known such a depth of silence around her; only her footsteps rang like chimes and her breath rasped in her throat. She knew that Anabel was no longer with her. *She doesn't want this*, Ellie thought. *She doesn't want me to leave her.* Stealthily she climbed the ladder to the lantern room, slowly lifted the latch to the lantern, and struck a match. Trembling, she dropped the match into the nest of feathers and twigs she had created inside the old lantern. Within seconds the flames spurted up, greedy for air. But she fed the lantern slowly, remembering her rapture when her bonfire took flame, and how rapidly she used up all her fuel in her excitement. *Take it steady, take it slow*, she told herself. *This light is going to save my life.*

The windows mirrored the flames into a spectacular dance, so the lantern room blazed with light. The more she fed the blaze, the more smoke poured out. She was in a trance, feeding, feeding the flame, twig by twig, feather by feather. Her eyes were streaming, her throat was burning, her lungs hurt, but still she fed the lamp, till nearly half her fuel was gone. She would wait until it had nearly burnt down and then feed it again. By this time the hatch was too hot for her to touch; she forced it down with the edge of her torch. Briefly the blaze sheared up again, like a glorious firework, and then the glass shattered with the heat.

Ellie crouched on the floor, screaming with fright, her hands clasped across her face. Hot shards of glass exploded in every direction. She backed away, groping for her torch, and then realised she must douse the fire before she left. She felt round on her hands and knees and found the pan of water that she had brought up earlier when she had come to clean the windows. She fumbled for the rag she had used, soaked it in the water, and covered the steaming little wormy flames that wriggled still in the broken lantern's base. Stinking smoke rose up, but she dipped the rag again and again into the pan and smothered the flames, the ashes, and finally the smoke.

'Stupid, stupid, stupid,' she kept moaning to herself. Tears of shock and frustration coursed down her sooty cheeks. 'Stupid, stupid, stupid.'

Miserable and sick, she walked slowly down the lighthouse steps and out into the night. She had lost her chance, her last chance, through stupidity and carelessness. In deep despair she walked down behind the back of the lighthouse towards Cormorant Cliff. The night was deeply black around her, but she didn't even switch her torch on. She didn't care any more what might happen to her.

Some gulls were still flying; white, luminous specks against the darkness. And then they were gone again. And back again, lit, as if they were caught in a searchlight. Dark again. Then lit again, and the white cliff as it curved inland in the keyhole cove was streaked with light; and the sea was strobe-lit, with glitters of foam; and the grass was bleached white; and then deep dark again. Light; dark again. A flash of light; there were gulls. Now they had gone.

It was like the flicker of an early black and white film; a lantern-show of silhouettes. Shadows, light; negative, positive.

She counted the seconds slowly. Light. Dark. One, two . . . fifteen. Light. Dark. One, two . . . fifteen. Every fifteen seconds. She knew what it was, and yet she dared not turn to look; not until she had to, not until the steady, sure rhythm of the flashing light was undeniable. She turned slowly. It was coming from the lighthouse. She counted again. Fifteen seconds between lights. But the lighthouse was no longer operated. It hadn't functioned since Guthrie lived on the island, thirty years ago.

CHAPTER TWENTY-SIX

George was sleeping at home, dreaming of Morag rising out of her deep coma like someone rising out of a sea, reaching towards him. And then her face changed and it wasn't Morag at all, it was Ellie, trying to tell him something, but when she opened her mouth no words came out, only a tiny, repeating ringing sound. He opened his eyes into darkness, and realised that the ringing sound was a phone downstairs, and he levered himself out of bed. He heard someone running down the stairs, the light being switched on, and then his father's voice, sleepy, then loud, questioning. George stumbled out of the room, trying to hear what his father was saying. The phone call ended as he joined his father downstairs.

'Dad? Is it the hospital?'

'It was Guthrie. From Kyle.'

'Guthrie?'

'He's had a call from a fisherman. He thought he saw a

light coming from the lighthouse. Guthrie thought you were messing about up there, and he rang to tell me. He was really angry. I couldn't get any sense out of him.'

'A light? But it doesn't work.'

'Exactly. Anyway, I told him it's nothing to do with you, because you're here.' He turned to go back upstairs. 'I thought it was the hospital too,' he said, weary. 'I thought it was your mother. She hasn't come home yet. I thought that Morag had had a relapse. I couldn't make any sense of what Guthrie was saying.'

'Dad.' George could hardly speak for the bewildered panic that was rising up in him. 'Listen, Dad. What if it's Ellie?'

'What do you mean? Ellie? Who on earth is Ellie?' His father's voice was fuddled. All he wanted to do was to go back to bed. George grabbed his arm.

'You know. I was trying to phone her house earlier.'

'The girl who went to the island with you?'

'What if she's still there? What if she's signalling for help?' He felt like crying. He couldn't bear the anger and bewilderment in his father's eyes. 'Guthrie can't have found my note. I left her behind, Dad.'

CHAPTER TWENTY-SEVEN

Ellie ran across the white and black strobing grass back towards the cottage, and flung herself inside, shivering.

She stood stock still in the doorway. Everything had changed. There was no longer a table by the window, but a bare bench pushed against the wall, with signs of a finished meal on it. A few candles were burning; logs crackling in the hearth, rushes were strewn on the bare floor. The door to one of the bedrooms was open; a hammock was slung from the beams. It was swinging slowly.

Trembling, she edged her way inside. This was somebody else's home; not hers, not George's or his family's. Anabel's home. A tartan shawl that she had never seen before was slung across a chair. She picked it up and wrapped it round her shoulders and then went over to the fire, warming herself, though it wasn't from the cold that she was shivering now. She had no idea what to do, or where to go. There was no sofa, no sleeping bag, nothing that was there before. Ah, but there was that tile on the wall, the rough childish sketching of the boat, the name misspelt. *Specter*. Now as her eyes got used to the shadows and glow in the room she noticed the black logbook, open, on the windowsill, next to a lit candle. She went over to it slowly, then sat down on the windowsill and picked up the book. The ink was still wet. Someone had just finished writing in it, and had left it there, she was sure, for her to read. She could see that the handwriting was large, almost printed, and that as it reached the end of the page it was stabbed onto the paper rather than written neatly, as if writing was too painful. She huddled herself against the cold window, and began to read.

July 20ᵗʰ, Eighteen hundred and twenty. A bright day, and the sky like bluebells, and skylarks filling the air with sound, and all is calm on the sea.

And I am so full of joy that my heart is bursting with it. For today my message came! I watched Old Guthrie's boat coming round into the shell beach, with his mussel baskets piled ready around him, and when he drew close to the shore he stood up in his boat that rocked like a baby's cradle and he put a wooden flute to his mouth and began to play a tune for me, and my heart it did soar like a white fulmar because I knew the tune and I knew what it meant, and I went dancing along the beach with the shells crunching and crackling under my feet. Haste to the Wedding it was, and I knew it well, hadn't I danced to it when I was a child and living every week with my grandmother in Kyle so I could be schooled? I lifted my skirts to my knees and flounced like a lady born. 'When, when?' I cried, and Old Guthrie shouted back, 'Tomorrow, lassie! Your Boy Adair has arranged with the minister to wed you this Sunday coming. Tomorrow on the evening tide he will come over for ye, and bring ye to Fish Green tae my mother's for the night. And the next day he will tak ye to the minister, and ye'll be a wedded woman!'

So he told me, and waved, and then he struck his oars into the sea again for to row round to the mussel beds on the wrack.

July 21st, Eighteen hundred and twenty. This is the day Boy said he would come to me. Since I got the message from Old Guthrie that he would be coming I am like a cat with jitters, and the merry jig he played to me has been spilling from my lips all day long. Haste to the wedding! I will! I will! Oh tide, come fast, come fast!

July 22nd. I can hardly write. No sleep have I slept,

no food nor drink have I taken, no breath have I breathed that is not trembling with sorrow. And this is what happened, and I still have no sense to make of it.

I was clean and dressed and ready, waiting for Boy Adair to bring his boat to me. Tide come, and wind rose sudden, and out of nowhere the wind brought the storm. Sea flung up waves as high as cliffs. I ran to Landlook, and there he was, far out on the sandbank. He was coming to me, he was coming, but why on foot? Why was he on the sandbank? He must know how treacherous it is. 'Boy!' I shouted. 'Go back. It's dangerous! Go back! Come tomorrow, don't try today!' Tide come sweeping round, fierce as horses, wild, wild things. I ran to the creek, oh my heart was drumming. I ran, I stumbled, fell, crawled in my wedding-clean skirts to bring my own boat to the water, to fetch my love safe to me. I rowed out from the creek with all my young girl's strength. I rowed to bring him safe across to the island. How I would do it, I did not know, for I cannot swim and nor can he, and the channels were filling fast with water that would swamp my boat and overturn her like a cockle shell, yet still I rowed for him. Then I saw a boat. Could I be mistook? Could it be Boy Adair after all, come to fetch me as he said he would? It *was coming round towards Landlook Point. But it was Old Man Guthrie who was rowing it, Guthrie, Guthrie, tumbling backwards and forward in it, lumbering up out of the waves like a whale. The sea it tossed the boat this way, that, and forced her on the rocks, and the great swell bore down on Guthrie as I watched. 'Save me! Help me! Anabel, save my life for pity's sake!' Old Guthrie was shouting. 'I saw his head go under, and his arms waving and helpless. 'Save me, Annie!'*

And save him I did, with all my body I rowed, with all my body I heaved him on my boat. And he lay gasping spewing groaning like a stinking fish, but a live one. I turned my boat and hauled to land. But the sandbanks, they was covered now. No Boy. No Boy there. No Boy there now. No Boy.

The chill of an unseen shadow fell across Ellie. Ice-cold fingers stroked her cheek. She woke from her trance of reading, startled, and dropped the book to the ground. The ghost-girl was standing in front of her. Her face was as white as the moon itself, her eyes deep-dark, her hair stained grey in that non-darkness, non-light. Ellie scrambled to her feet, and the girl clasped her, cold hand in cold hand.

'Now! It is time!'

Ellie tried to pull herself away, but her hand was locked inside Anabel's grip.

'You will help me now.' Anabel pulled Ellie with her out of the cottage. Still Ellie tried to wrench herself away, but the ghost-girl's grasp was like a handcuff of ice that had frozen into her bone; nothing she did would free her, and there was nothing she could do but run by her side, gasping with fright and pain as she was half-dragged over the hummocks and boulders and along the moon-white track towards Landlook Point.

'Look,' Anabel said, her voice ragged with grief. The ghost-girl slipped her hand out of Ellie's and together they gazed out to the distant sandbank. It was clearly lit now by shafts of light, black against the white gleam of sand and the turmoiled current that coursed round it always. A figure stood out there, hand lifted, and the tide was turning fast, fast, towards him, snaking through the channels of soft sand.

The ghost-girl turned her pale face towards Ellie, linked her now with an arm round Ellie's waist. 'Take me to him.'

Ellie shook her head, trying to break away. 'I can't. I can't.'

'I never saw him there again till you came here. You've brought him back to me. Bring him to my arms.'

'How? I don't know how.'

'You must,' Anabel insisted. 'Tomorrow is my wedding day.'

And now Ellie was running again alongside Anabel, and it was no longer in her to resist. She was running and gasping for breath, she was hauling herself up the Height, over the crest of it, never stopping, clasping the ghost-girl's hand in her own hand. Now they were slithering side by side, slipping and skidding down the bank to the creek, down to the rotting black boat *Spectre*. The tide had filled the creek; the boat had risen to the bank. Anabel stepped off the bank, up to her thighs in black, swirling water, and pushed the gunwales of the boat until it nosed away from her into the tide. She scrambled into it, held out her hand to Ellie, and helped her in. Anabel turned to her, her face lit with laughter, her eyes bright with joy.

Still Ellie had no idea what she was expected to do. Anabel picked up the oars and rowed, head lifted high, as she must have rowed that night nearly two hundred years ago to meet her young husband-to-be. Ellie clung to the sides as the boat tipped and bobbed out of the creek and finally into the open sea. At first it was clear that the rowing was no effort, the tide was flooding so fast and carrying them along with it. They streamed round the island to Landlook Point, and Ellie looked about fearfully for rocks. Surely they were there, and over there, and here, black as sharks, rearing their jagged heads out of the water, there, and over there, where the foam licked and creamed and the spray fountained high, surely they would crack the bones of the boat and splinter it to shards?

But the ghost-girl never paused, and Ellie realised that she knew every inch of the sea around Wild Island, every rock and current. She steered the boat easily and steadily round Landlook Point and headed out towards the sandbanks. And as she rowed she sang; though Ellie couldn't hear her she could see her lips moving, and she knew it was the tune that Anabel wanted to dance to at her own wedding.

Ellie edged forward in the boat and turned herself round until she was sitting alongside Anabel. She took one of the oars from her and rowed grimly and purposefully. She was intent now on helping her. Maybe the ghost-girl's aim was to row to Kyle, and if it was, then it would be the means of Ellie's salvation. And if she was truly rowing for the sandbank, then there was nothing Ellie could do to stop her anyway. She didn't have the strength or the skill to turn the boat round and head back to the island against the rush of the incoming tide. It was hardly any effort to row with the tide; it was better than just sitting helplessly watching from the slippery bench at the front of the boat. Anabel turned her head briefly towards Ellie. Her hair flicked away from her face and in that brief moment Ellie saw that she was happy. *If I help her*, Ellie thought, *maybe she will help me to get to land. There's no way I can row to Kyle on my own. She will row me to land, and I'll be free.*

But this is madness, she told herself. *It's the madness that George told me about, the madness of keepers trapped on the island, the madness of the exiled king. How can I be in a boat with a ghost-girl, rowing alongside her?* Yet the shower of spray soaked her, the oar was firm in her hands.

The sky was lightening fast now, streaked with apricot and sapphire as the sun rose. It was a brilliant and beautiful dawn. Ellie kept glancing over her shoulder towards the sandbank. It was gleaming now with the sky's reflected light. A thin skin of water was already streaming across it. The boy was standing there still, arm raised, his image puzzling into the water that was seeping round his feet. 'Anabel,' she whispered, 'he's so near.' She couldn't help herself; she was engaged in Anabel's task. She wanted to rescue Boy Adair.

The ghost-girl, too, kept turning her head to look at him, whispering under her breath, tears streaming down her cheeks, 'Let me be in time. Let me just hold him. Let me be in time.'

As soon as the black boat nosed its way into the channel that surrounded the sandbank, it began to twitch and twirl in a kind of frenzied and uncontrollable dance. Ellie felt her oar being snatched out of her hand by the strength of the current. She grabbed out at it, but it took all her strength to hold it in its place in the rowlock. Anabel forced the boat round by heaving on her own oar. They were yards away now from where Boy Adair had been standing, but Ellie couldn't see him any longer because he was behind her on the bank, and she was working desperately to keep the boat steady. Anabel kept glancing at him over her shoulder. Her hair lashed in wild strands across her face. The boat struggled like a frightened horse; it could not edge into the current; always it was forced away.

'We'll never make it,' Ellie shouted at Anabel. 'The current's too strong.'

Anabel took no notice of her now. It was as if Ellie was no longer there. 'Adair! Boy!' she screamed. 'Swim to me! Swim!' Ellie caught a brief glimpse of the young man on the bank as the boat lurched and plunged on the edge of the current. He never moved. It was as if he was locked to the spot in terror, while the water rose up to his waist, and kept on rising.

'We must go back,' Ellie shouted to Anabel. 'Go back, or leave the sandbanks and try to head for Kyle. We must get help.'

Nothing made sense. This moment was as real as if it was happening now, as if a flesh and blood girl was sitting beside her in the rocking boat, as if her flesh and blood sweetheart was about to drown in front of her eyes. But Anabel had died, many years ago. Boy Adair had drowned. Ellie knew that.

'I cannot leave him there,' Anabel moaned. 'Nor can I swim to him, nor can he swim to me.'

Ellie stared at her, frightened now beyond any fear that she had experienced on the island. She knew now for sure why the ghost-girl had brought her out here to the sandbank.

'You can swim. You can bring him to me,' Anabel said. 'Let me hold him just one time.'

Did she say it at all? Did she scream it above the roaring sound of the waves, or did Ellie hear it in her head?

'No. No. It's too dangerous. Nobody can swim through this current.'

There is menace and fury in the sea.

And I am afraid of it.

The boat had swung round so they were facing the ghost boy. He was less than ten metres away from them. The water was rising to his hips now, and still he didn't move. He was a ghost, Ellie knew that, and yet she could not sit there and watch him drown. She knew what she was expected to do, and she had no way of resisting it. It was as if the ghost-girl had transferred all her own longing and anguish to Ellie. There was no turning back, and there was no refusing Anabel's plea.

'Bring him to me.'

Nor was there was any time left to pause for thought or reason or fear or doubt. Ellie stood up unsteadily, stepped to the side of the boat, and plunged into the water. Her feet groped for the ground and found none. The current zipped her sideways. She flailed out with her arms, and felt herself being sucked below the waves, floundering helplessly, flung back up, gasping for air. She was whirled and sucked and spat into air again, waves slammed her this way and that, and there was no strength left in her to fight the sea.

'Take hold. Take hold of me.'

She was blind with the wash of water across her face, but

somehow she twisted herself towards the voice and flung up her arms and caught hold of the boy's hands, gripped them and felt his grasp on hers tighten, like a limpet to a rock. She turned her head, and saw that Anabel was leaning out of the boat towards her. She was just a dim shape inside the swell of water, hands outstretched.

'Take him. Take him now!' Ellie's body was flung and swung under and up, up, and down to green depths, still holding fast. She felt herself slipping away from him, fingertips just touching. She felt he was being hauled away from her into the black boat.

'Mum!' she shouted. 'Mum! Help me!'

'Don't let go,' the voice urged. 'I have you. I've got you now.'

And then his fingertips touched hers again, his hands closed round her own, his grasp was firm and strong. Tighter, tighter, he hauled on her, and up she rose, heaved towards blinding yellow light and up and up again and into the gasp of air.

CHAPTER TWENTY-EIGHT

When Ellie opened her eyes again she was lying in the bottom of the boat. She retched, and somebody half-lifted her and rolled her over on her side, stroked her hair, held her hand.

'You're all right. I'm sorry. I'm so sorry. You're fine now. I've got you safe.'

She struggled to sit up. George was leaning over her, supporting her with both his arms round her. She looked up, bewildered. His father, Bill, was on the other side of her, holding out a blanket. George rolled it over her. At the tiller sat Guthrie, grim as ever. Ellie closed her eyes again, trying to remember what had happened, trying to work out why she was lying in Guthrie's boat, *Miss Tweedie*. She shuddered, and George pulled her closer to him, but again she struggled to sit up.

'Are the others safe?'

'The others? There aren't any others, Ellie.'

'In the black boat.'

'There's no boat there,' Guthrie said firmly.

'There's no-one else, Ellie.'

'No-one. Nothing,' Bill assured her. 'Just close your eyes. We'll have you safe in bed soon. Safe and warm and dry.'

As soon as they reached Kyle, George lifted Ellie out of the boat and carried her into his father's car. He tucked the blanket round her and sat beside her as Bill drove them to Aunt Izzie's house. Izzie was there already, waiting anxiously for them. She phoned for the local doctor and helped Ellie into a warm, comforting bath. By the time the doctor arrived, Ellie was snug in one of Izzie's nighties and warm in bed with a hot water bottle. George was sitting by her bed, watching her helplessly as she slipped in and out of sleep. When Doctor Fleming came into the room Izzie packed George off downstairs to sit with Guthrie.

'She was lucky,' Guthrie said. 'I don't know how you managed to spot her the way you did, struggling over to the sandbank. Poor lassie, she should never have been on that island. I tried to tell you.'

'I know that. I know,' George groaned. 'It was all my fault.'

'Aye, but I should have stopped you taking her there.'

'You weren't to blame. You couldn't have known what was going to happen.'

'Aye. Maybe so. Maybe no.'

They sat in gloomy silence listening to the murmur of voices upstairs. Bill was in the kitchen, trying to remember his way round his sister's cupboards so he could make something like breakfast for them all, muttering to himself, clanging dishes and cutlery in a spectacularly failing attempt to pretend that everything was all right. When the doctor and Izzie came down the stairs he spilt the contents of a packet of cereal over the floor tiles, and crunched over them in his socks to stand anxiously in the doorway.

'Do we need to send for an ambulance?' he asked.

The doctor shook her head. 'No. She'll be fine. She's a brave wee girl.'

'But how is she?' George asked. He was conscious of the fact that only hours ago he was asking the same thing about Morag.

'Well, she appears to be surprisingly fine, physically. She's very fit and strong in spite of being such a slender wee thing.'

'She's a dancer,' George muttered. He could recall every word of their conversations together on the island. All the long, high-speed, worried journey from home to Kyle last night in his father's car, he had been remembering what he and Ellie had said to each other; their awkwardness, their unexpected laughter, their shy attempts at friendship. He had never stopped thinking how sweet she was, and how rude to her he had been.

'Well, there you are,' Dr Fleming said. It was obvious that she was angry with George and Guthrie. She turned away from them to speak only to Bill and Izzie. 'It's quite surprising to me, but there is absolutely no damage done to her heart or her lungs. She's breathing perfectly normally. She's as well as anyone could be after an experience like that. I see no reason to send her to the hospital for a check-up; she's shocked, but she's well. She needs rest, lots of rest, and personally I think it's better to keep her comfortable in bed here than to put her through a long trip to the hospital.'

'I agree,' said Aunt Izzie. 'And as you know, I have some nursing experience, Doctor Fleming.' She put her hands behind her back, proud. 'I would like to take care of her.'

'Good. She's in excellent hands. I'm quite happy. I'll come back this afternoon and check up on her, and you can phone me any time if you're worried. I feel she'll be fine.' The doctor folded away her notes, and then eyed George and Guthrie in turn over the top of her glasses. 'That's what I have to say about her physical condition.'

'It's a great relief to hear you say all this,' Bill began, but Doctor Fleming held up her hand to silence him.

'Apart from nearly drowning, the young woman has been through a terrible experience. She was alone on that island for several days. She has no real idea how long. She felt she had been abandoned, and she had no idea why, or what to do about it, and I feel that is why she made the unbelievably brave decision to try to swim to the sandbanks and to attempt to beat the tide for Kyle. It would be a terrible, terrible time for anyone, to be alone like that with no hope of rescue, let alone for a susceptible girl of her age.'

George groaned and put his head in his hands. Aunt Izzie sat down next to him, her arm across his shoulders.

'Come on now, George. You must not blame yourself. We've been through all that already.'

'Aye,' Guthrie sighed deeply. He stood up and walked over to the window, and stood with his arms folded across his chest, watching the sea, and beyond that, the dark island. 'That's not the half of it,' he muttered.

The doctor nodded. 'You will know perhaps what she was trying to tell me, Guthrie, and it's you who needs to speak to her, but not yet. I forbid you to. The last thing the girl needs to see at the moment is your gloomy face.'

They had known each other all their lives, after all, from the time they went to the local school. Both their families had lived in Kyle for centuries.

'I'll speak to her when she's well enough. Aye.' Guthrie sighed again. 'I think she has a queer tale to tell, that no-one will believe but me.'

'Can I go up to her?' George asked.

'Certainly not. I should think you're the other last person she wants to see at the moment,' Dr Fleming said briskly. Aunt Izzie squeezed George's shoulder again. 'She needs sleep. There's only one person she wants to see.'

'Her dad?' suggested George.

'Indeed not. She wants her mother.'

CHAPTER TWENTY-NINE

The tide was just beginning to turn when George slipped away unnoticed from Aunt Izzie's house and sprinted down to the shore. He ran along the beach until he came to the lifeboat station, where he had left *Sprite* pulled up on the shore days ago. He would have to be quick, he knew that. He could have asked Guthrie to take him in *Miss Tweedie*, but this was something he wanted to do on his own, for Ellie's sake. He rigged *Sprite* quickly, hauled her down the white sand, and leapt aboard as he was pushing her out. He skimmed rapidly to the island and beached cleanly, jumped down and pulled his boat ashore. He ran up to the lighthouse cottage and was about to run straight through to the room that Ellie had been sleeping in when he saw his own sleeping bag spread on the couch, with her T-shirt rolled up on top of it. He smiled, imagining her there, bravely sleeping through the mice scrabblings. He found her rucksack, scooped up her sketchbook, pens and paints, odd bits of clothing, and at the last minute, the black book on the windowsill, which she must have been reading. He checked that her mobile was in the pocket of the rucksack, slung it over his shoulder and hurried back to *Sprite*. The tide was ebbing, but he still had time to get to Kyle if he was careful and speedy. As soon as he arrived he hauled his boat up onto shore and turned on Ellie's mobile. There was enough life in it to allow him to dip through the menu to the contact list. There it was. *Mum*. He fished out his own mobile from his pocket and, shaking uncontrollably now, took a deep breath, and keyed in the number.

Ellie slept through the day and the night. When she woke up, her mother was sitting by her bed. Ellie heaved a sigh of relief and smiled. She crept her hand out from under her quilt and grasped her mother's. 'I'm fine,' she whispered. 'I'm fine now.'

Eventually, between sleeping and sleeping again, between quiet visits from people she knew and scarcely knew and didn't know at all, she was always aware that her mother was there at her bedside, stroking her forehead. Occasionally, hovering in the doorway anxiously, she saw George.

'He really wants to talk to you,' her mother said. 'Will you let him?'

Ellie nodded and sat up in the bed. George tiptoed into the room like a clumsy giraffe. 'Ellie,' he whispered. 'You probably thought I'd just abandoned you. None of this should have happened – but please believe me, it was all a terrible mistake.'

She closed her eyes, not wanting to look at him; too full of raw emotion. 'Okay. Tell me.'

And stumblingly he told her about Morag's strange, life-threatening illness and the message he had sent to Guthrie with an envelope of money. Guthrie had since collected it from the holiday cottage next door to his own, and George produced it as proof and put it on the table by the bed.

Ellie frowned, trying to make sense of all that. She stored it away to mull over later. 'I'm glad Morag's better,' was all she could say to him, before she turned away and slept again, and he, helpless and miserable, stood up quietly and left her.

When she woke up again it was just her mother in the room. They ate together and then her mother helped her to dress and to come to sit in a chair by the window.

'You've had an awful time, Ellie. I don't intend to rush you but the sooner we can leave this place and go home, the better it will be for you.'

'Where's Angus?' Ellie asked, remembering the wedding, the honeymoon, the bitterness she had felt. None of that seemed to matter any more.

'Don't worry about him. We've found a very nice place to stay in the village and he's happily exploring the coast path walks while I'm with you. He'll be bird-watching.'

'He should talk to George. He knows a lot about birds.' She saw her mother's brief, surprised smile. 'He taught me a lot on the island. And then I learned the names of some, off by heart, when I was on my own.' She lowered her head. 'It seemed like forever, Mum.'

'I know my love. I know. It must have been unbearable for you. How brave you've been. I think I understand some of what you've been through, but not all by any means.' She brought Ellie's rucksack over to the chair and took out the sketchbook. 'Ellie. I've been looking through this. Your work is wonderful. I think you're right, and you should go to Art College when you leave school if you still want to. You're very, very talented. But I don't understand a lot of the paintings. Maybe you'll tell me about them.'

Ellie nodded. She reached out for the sketchbook and closed it up, then let it lie on her lap. She swallowed hard, wiping tears away with her free hand.

'I haven't read the notes you made, because they were addressed to your dad. Will you tell me what happened? I think you're ready to talk about it now. Even if it makes you cry. It doesn't matter. Tell me.'

So, little by little, Ellie told her mother the story of how George had left her alone on the island. Then, stumblingly, she told her about Anabel. Whether her mother believed her or not, it was impossible to tell. She just kept listening and nodding and stroking Ellie's hand.

'My poor girl,' she said, when Ellie had finished. 'We're all blaming ourselves. It's really my fault. I shouldn't have left you behind to go away with Angus. It was selfish and thoughtless of me.'

This was the time, Ellie knew, to ask the question that she had never dared put into words before. 'I want to ask you something, Mum. When Dad went to Cornwall – did he go on his own?'

'No. He didn't.' There was a long, painful silence. 'He has a new partner.'

Ellie thought back wildly. Dad had been different for the past year. He had been happy, sad, thoughtful, angry. So had her mother.

'He has a new life, and so have I. We both have new loves.

Don't blame him, Ellie. It shouldn't have happened, but it did. He still loves you, you know that, don't you?'

Ellie nodded. 'I think so.'

'I couldn't talk to you about it at first. I tried to hide it from you, and then in the last few months things happened too quickly. I met Angus, and he made life better for me. Your father made his plans, and we didn't tell you about any of it because of your exams. If we'd treated you like a grown-up instead of like a child, none of this would have happened to you. Maybe you could phone him later. He needs to know what's happened. I can't bear to think what you've been through.' She shuddered. Her eyes shone with tears, then she shook her head and tried to smile at her daughter. 'So blame me, and your dad, but don't blame George. The poor boy is in pieces, millions of pieces. Please let him talk to you again. Give him a proper chance to say he's sorry, Ellie.'

At that moment there was a tap on the door, and Guthrie put his face round. 'If I don't speak to the lassie, I'll burst like a piece of bladderwrack,' he told them. 'And, besides, I need to be gone with the tide soon.'

Ellie nodded at her mother.

'All right,' her mother said. She wiped her eyes. 'Come on in, Guthrie. I'll give you ten minutes.'

Guthrie tiptoed in, with George hovering in the doorway behind him.

'May I come in too, Ellie?' George asked. He slipped a bar of chocolate out of his pocket and put it on the arm of Ellie's chair. Ellie's mother smiled and squeezed her daughter's hand, then moved away to make room for them both.

The visitors sat themselves on either side of the window. Ellie was conscious of a glow of warmth as George sat down next to her, though she kept her face away from him and stared across the water to the island. She was still thinking about what Mum had told her. Her mother set to quietly tidying the room. She was not prepared to leave her daughter for a moment.

'I've a tale to tell ye,' said Guthrie. 'Concerning an ancestor of mine, by the same name as myself, Guthrie.' He glanced at George. 'This is not a Kyle rumour, though there are many of those about ancestors of mine. This is an item of family history that my grandfather gave to me, about his own great-grandfather, and which we are sorely grieved about and have told no-one beyond the family. It concerns my ancestor, and a wee lassie of the island. And it also concerns a young crofter named Adair – known locally as Boy, even when he was grown tae be a young man, having the same name as his father. Boy Adair was known to be waiting to wed the lighthouse keeper's daughter on Wild Island.'

'That was Anabel,' said Ellie. Still she didn't look at Guthrie but at the distant island, looming and losing itself in the wreathing mists.

'So you know that? You know the story?' Guthrie asked.

'Some of it, yes. I saw her.'

Guthrie let out a long, slow sigh. 'You saw Anabel? The ghost of Wild Island?' he said slowly.

Ellie nodded. She couldn't put her story into words for them. Not yet.

'I have never seen her myself. But some say they have. So you saw her.'

There was a long silence in the room.

'Were you frightened?' George asked.

Ellie bit her lip. How could she ever tell them how frightened she had been? She could only think now about Anabel in her boat, leaning out with her arms stretched towards the boy on the sandbank. Her eyes welled up with tears. 'I don't know all her story. I know she was waiting to marry Boy, and he never came.'

'That's the way it was,' Guthrie said. 'My ancestor visited the island on most tides, for he was a musselman, and the mussels on Wild Island are the best on any part of the Scottish coast. And so it was my ancestor who took her the message that the next day, Boy Adair would be crossing the sea in his own wee boat to bring her back with him to Fish Green, so that they would be married in the kirk in his own parish. But on the very day that Boy Adair was to fetch his Anabel to shore, Guthrie, my ancestor, was setting out for the mussel beds on the island and found that his boat was leaking. And he borrowed Adair's boat without asking, thinking to be home with the incoming tide so the boy could keep his tryst that day.'

'But a sudden storm rose up,' interrupted Ellie.

'Aye, that's what I was told. And my ancestor couldn't bring the wee boat back to Kyle. It wasn't a true fishing boat, it wasn't meant for heavy seas. He went back to Wild Island for shelter in the cove.'

'And Boy Adair tried to walk across to the sandbank, to wave to Anabel, to let her know that he would come if he could.' Ellie turned to Guthrie. 'I know what happened next. Anabel saw him there. It's in the logbook that I found in the lighthouse. She set off in her own rowing boat to bring him over from the sandbank.'

'I didn't know that. But I know that my ancestor Guthrie

broke the wee boat that he had taken from Adair. It smashed on the rocks. He was thrown into the sea and would have lost his life, but Anabel heard his cries and rescued him. She saved his life.'

'And Boy Adair drowned. She saved Old Man Guthrie's life, but she was too late to save Adair's. It's all in the logbook.'

'The young man was never seen again. That is the story that my grandfather told me. Anabel stayed on the island all her life, refused to move from the place, waiting for him still to come to her, because his body never was found.'

'I know it's true,' Ellie said. 'She wrote it all down. I found the logbook in the lighthouse. There's lots of mentions about her watching out for him.'

Guthrie frowned. 'I've never seen a logbook in the lighthouse.'

'I found a book,' George said. 'I didn't realise what it was, but I put it in your rucksack along with your sketchbook and stuff.'

'Here,' Ellie's mother said. She brought the rucksack over to him and he rummaged through it and pulled out the black logbook. Ellie leafed through it, frowning. Guthrie leaned over her shoulder, anxious to see what might have been said about his ancestor.

'It's not there!' Ellie exclaimed. She flicked over page after page. The diary entries logging Anabel's activities as lighthouse keeper were still there, but the scrawled notes about waiting for Boy had all gone. 'I can't believe it! They were there, they were definitely there. I read them all. I saw her writing one of them.'

'Don't worry about it,' George said. He took the logbook gently away from her. 'It doesn't matter.'

'But it does. How else would I have known the story? Let me look again. You think I was trying to get away from the island when you found me? I was helping Anabel. She made me take her to Adair. She wanted to hold him, that's what she told me. We knew he was drowning, and we tried to save him. You don't believe me, do you?'

'I – I don't know what to believe. But I think you should have a rest,' George said. He looked warningly at Guthrie. 'She's tired. We shouldn't have told her the story yet.'

Mum put her arms round Ellie and held her tight.

'It's all right,' said Ellie. 'I'm glad Guthrie told me about his ancestor. So I know the whole story now.'

'It is not something that our family is proud of, ye understand,' Guthrie mumbled, awkward now. 'It is a bad piece of history, but it needed to be told today.' He pushed his chair back and stood up, shaking his head, then he bent down to Ellie.

'I just wanted to say, Ellie' – he dropped his voice to a whisper that everyone could hear – 'what ye have done has put an end to the story. You've brought Boy Adair to his lassie's arms. It's over now. Do ye understand? Over.'

He grasped her hand, and she nodded. She leant her head back against the chair, closed her eyes, and smiled. Over. Yes. Over. Over for both of them. She and Anabel had helped each other. She was safe with her family, and Anabel was at peace.

Guthrie crept out of the room on tiptoe, and George followed him down to the front door.

'I don't understand any of that,' he said. 'I don't know whether to believe her or not.'

'Ye don't need to understand, but you do need to believe. I do, with all my old bones I do. Yon lassie is the bravest I've ever come across, I'm telling you that. I have heard people say they felt strange things happening on the island, but I've never seen anything to make me think it was true. That's why I didn't want the lassie to go there in the first place. If there was something peculiar going on, it was for the family to find, not strangers. I didn't want to believe my island was

263

haunted, you understand, George? She has done what no other person who has stepped on that island has ever dared to do. She believed in the ghosts. She's brought peace to the place.'

CHAPTER THIRTY

On the day Ellie was leaving, she and George walked down to the shore together. Her mother and Angus came out of the Guest House they were staying in and stood hand in hand, waiting for Ellie to join them at their car. The incoming tide was just lapping the jetty.

'What will you do now?' Ellie asked.

'I'm going to wait at Izzie's for Morag and Mum to arrive. Then, if Morag's up to it, we'll go over to the island. I'm going grape-picking in France after that. Working holiday, with some friends from school, before we all go off to uni.'

'I'm going to spend a few days with Mum and Angus,' Ellie paused. 'Then I'm going to Cornwall to see Dad.'

'Good idea. Forget about all this, if you can.'

They looked across at Wild Island, wreathed as always in mist, with the green of the Height gleaming through from time to time.

'It's a magic place,' said Ellie. 'I still think so.'

'Would you ever go back there?'

'Not yet. One day. Perhaps.'

'With us?'

'I certainly wouldn't go on my own!'

She looked away. Her mother and Angus waved, then paused, waiting for her to say goodbye to George before she joined them.

'The tide's coming in,' he said. 'Look at the waves, wagging their scallies at us.'

She nodded, smiling, hugging his words to herself. *Our joke*, she thought. *Don't share it with anyone else. Please.*

'Ellie. I've got your mobile number. Do you mind if I text you sometime?'

'I'd mind if you didn't. But you won't be able to, when you're on the island.'

'Then I'll sail over every day on *Sprite*, and I'll phone you from Kyle. Will that do?'

He touched her hand, briefly, warm, and then she caught both his hands in hers and held them tight, looking up at him.

'It'll do,' she said, smiling. 'For now.'